Last Kiss At Midnight

Rachel Roy

Copyright

Table of Contents

Chapter 1 - Brigittia

"**B**ut look, it's an unmasking at midnight! How romantic! You dance and spend all evening with someone you don't even know and then everyone will unmask at midnight! Usually, we all drop our masks after an hour and then just use them as a fashion accessory." My cousin's face was all lit up with excitement and joy for me, not to mention happy envy about the invitation.

"Yeah, romantic."

"You don't sound excited."

"I'm not."

"But whhhhyyyyy? This is so amazing, and you were invited!"

"Hmm, just not my thing, I guess." Truthfully, I was remembering why this particular masquerade ball was hosted every five years - the Quinquennial Masquerade Ball. It was in the history books that I had studied, but not the ones studied by my cousin. It wasn't nearly as romantic when you understood the reasons for the ball.

Sure you get a fancy invite, and everyone goes crazy finding you the most divine dress and mask. You have guards that escort you to the ball. Depending on the year you get a clue about your partner in the invitation, or some years it's when you come in through the door. These partners have been chosen for you, but you don't know until you find your match at the ball. Maybe you're both bumblebees or frogs or whatever. And then there is the grand unmasking at midnight to learn who your partner really is. Yeah, sounds great.

"Ooh, we'll have so much fun picking out your dress! You know your mom will convince your dad to buy you anything. You should get new jewelry too to complement your mask.-"

I cut off her gushing, "I'm not going."

"Umm, what?" My little cousin, Titania, opened her eyes wide in surprise. For her, this was the best invitation one could ever receive. This was the ball to attend. It only happened twice in a decade.

"No. I don't want to go."

"But it will be so amazing. It's a *once in a lifetime* ball!" She almost wailed the last part. She was right. You only attended once.

"You have to go!" Well, there was that. She had no idea how right she was. "I can't wait until I get invited. I hope I get invited."

I bit my tongue. I know it was *The Event* and hugely exciting from her perspective. But she wasn't in line to the throne. She didn't have all the private history classes that I had. She didn't know. Hopefully, she would never know. And I couldn't tell her, even if I wanted to. The Auld Magic swirls around some things and it is heavily entwined with this. I could kick and scream and throw a fit, but really, there wasn't a choice. Not for me. Not for any of the invitees.

"Maybe you're right." I softened my voice. There was no reason for Titania to be distraught.

"Of course I'm right. I know you would rather read a book, or practice with your daggers, Brigittia, but leave this sort of thing to me. You need more social interactions and we are going to make you the belle of this ball!"

Oh goody.

"We'll design you the perfect dress and mask. We'll find a fan for you too, just in case it's unbearably hot with so many people since you can't take off your mask. Ooh, if we design you a green mask, we can drape your throat with emeralds. Blue could be sapphires. White and diamonds would be too common, maybe rubies, and they could drip from around your throat right down into your cleavage. You do have good tits."

"You know, dripping rubies sounds good. Covered in symbolic blood. I like it." *But not, dear cousin, for why you might think.*

"Oh goody, we can even have you carry some fake daggers encrusted with jewels since you like them so-"

"Umm, why fake ones?"

"Oh, you silly!" she laughed in my face like I was the brainless one. "You know actual weapons aren't allowed there."

I might have forgotten that rule. Or was it a rule or just an expectation? That was important to find out.

I might need more time here in the practice rings to burn off this nervous tension.

"Rough day coming or rough night had?" asked Thorian, my trainer. Apparently, my face gives it all away.

"Both."

"Ahh. Time to work then." This is one thing I love about Jonas. First, he's been training me nearly since I could walk and he has an amazing understanding of my ability and how to push me to be my best. But because he's known me for so long, he also can read me better than anyone. He could waste time asking me questions and trying to solve the issue, but he doesn't waste the time. Later we'll talk, now we sweat.

"Alright, lass, give me three laps 'round the building to loosen up. You're tighter than I've near ever seen you. Then do you want hand to hand or blade work?"

"Ugh." I groan, but I know he's right. I'm too tight to do anything yet and running can stretch out these muscles that I've been holding so tight. "Whichever, surprise me."

"Well, are ye mad at one person in particular, or a group?"

"The world."

"Right then, off you go. Stretch that neck as ye run. Drop yer arms and swing them, eh?" He looks at me with expectation.

"Yes, Thorian." I don't have to enjoy it, and we both know it. I start off jogging the first side of the building to limber up and building up speed as I go to a steady, thrumming pace. Thorian only lifts an eyebrow as I go for an extra lap. He doesn't try to stop me.

"Ready now, lass?" He asks as I come to a rest before him, hardly breathing hard, but with a light sheen of sweat on my forehead and on my back.

"Let's do it."

He hands me a short blade and back scabbard. I rarely wear anything on my back where I have to draw it up over my head. It's awkward and leaves a huge opening if you have been caught by surprise.

"I figure yer already in a pisspoor mood. We might as well practice one of the things ye don't like. Why ruin another day later?" He has a point.

I shrug into the scabbard and awkwardly slide the blade in. Then plant my feet about shoulder width apart and shift my weight to the outside of my feet for better balance.

We watch each other as he circles. We know he'll swing first as the purpose of this isn't so much my blade work as it is to pull the sword when I need it. Suddenly, he ducks and rolls, pulling his blade as he comes up beside me. I spin and sidestep, but my balance is slightly off as I try to unsheathe at the same time. Most people watching might not have noticed, but Thorian is watching for it and bumps the back of my knee as he comes up. My balance dips more and I only manage a sloppy parry. His swing is solid though and reverberates up my arm.

"Again," he says neutrally.

We re-sheath our blades and stand ready again. This time he attacks with a false punch and then a kick, pulling his blade as he ducks down away from my punch delivered as I blocked and turned his kick. Now he has his blade and I haven't pulled mine. I quickly back step to put space between us as I pull my blade, but he's fast and slides the tip of his blade against my left arm as I bring my elbow down, blocking my face and still haven't gotten my blade extended.

"Worse. Again."

Again and again we move through scenarios of his attacking and me drawing my blade. There are a few that I do well, but mostly I am a sweating, frustrated mess.

"Enough, go get some water," he finally says. "We'll do some dancing next and bring yer back to a better mood."

"Finally," I grunt. I know this work is for my own good. I just painfully showed why I need it, but that doesn't make my inabilities less frustrating.

"Good, now while we dance," Thorian chose his stance and held his light sword, tip down, "list all the poisons you know that may be added to one's drink."

Now this would be fun. I love blade to blade combat, especially as we throw in kicks and rolls too. Adding in concentrating on poisons at the same time would add a challenge. As with every blade, balance was key.

The ring was soon ringing with steel against steel as we blocked and parried each other while I thought out loud about which poisons would have no taste in liquid or which liquids could hide their taste, but also wouldn't affect color or texture.

"Rhinesblade berries would be the perfect poison, with no color or taste, except that they thicken most drinks."

"Excellent," Thorian wouldn't praise me with superfluous language. He was genuinely happy that I had learned a new poison and its characteristics. "What else?"

Was nothing ever enough for him?

Chapter 2 - Thomas

"**I** understand it is a requirement, Father. I don't understand why *I* am required to go." I sounded like a petulant child because I was keeping such a tight rein on my anger. I respected my father, but this was a ridiculous request.

"You know very well that the herds numbers are down-"

"Of course," I ground out quietly.

"And," he continued, holding up a finger, "this does two things for us: we gain their protection when you marry the daughter, as well as the political persuasion that they carry. We need to bolster our power any way we can."

"I understand that, Father. And I understand we need a guaranteed fertile marriage - I appreciate your faith in me to stud an heir, by the way. But, what I don't understand is why ME? I'm second in line to the throne. Not first. I am not a warrior, which would best suit their clan. Why me?"

"Ahh, son." The broad shoulders drooped for just a moment and he murmured, "You're an adult now, you might want to forget that phrase." Then stronger he asked, "You remember your uncle, my brother?"

I took a step back. The sadness of his posture had given way to the steely strength of our family. "Yeah." There really wasn't anything to add to that. Father had been the second son as well, but when his brother was assassinated, he became the reigning Council Leader of the Greater Herds. "Right, sorry."

"Son, we need this alliance. And I understand she is a sweet girl. Her mother has raised many healthy children, but has insisted that they not only know how to raise a family, that they understand politics, and have a love of learning. This girl, I understand, loves to read. You should be able to have conversations in common at least as you get to know each other. You sound similar. She's young and strong, healthy, smart,-"

"-and my perfect fated mate. Yeah, I get it." I huffed angrily, but my father knew me well enough to see that I could see the reason in his words. "I get it. It's best for our herd for me to make alliances. And I know you did your best to find me a companion I will like. Thank you, Father."

He nodded his head.

"But," I added, it doesn't mean I have to like it. I will treat her with kindness; she likely has no more choice than I, but I do not have to celebrate this forced marriage."

"That is fair enough," for once he agreed with me without a lecture.

"And no, she had no choice. None of you heir-apparents had a voice in the arrangements, as far as we know. This was done family by family to protect our lines and to protect our people. We all have had dwindling populations, which in turn has made us all weaker. These alliances will bring fresh blood into our families and link us together in new political ways. It is strategic, I promise you. But we also tried to find pairings of lifetime happiness, or at least contentment. I do think you will like her."

"What else do you know about her, then?"

"She is a beautiful fae girl your age. I hear she has reddish brown hair, similar to yours, but a little darker. She has been trained with blades and archery, but prefers to negotiate with wit rather than blade. The girl has a pet wolf, whom may like to mate with yours and we can have two revived bloodlines, hey?"

I know he was trying to put things in a good light. I know it could be much, much worse. But why would I want an arranged marriage when all I wanted was peaceful happiness?

"Father says that she is a sweet girl. Which I guess I'm happy about. But this is still difficult for me. I thought I could travel and learn about the world. Then meet a girl and fall in love and I would be able to choose whom I would marry." Thomas had been brushing his horse quite gently when he started, but by the end of the tirade, his horse, Willow, kept sidestepping to buffer the brush strokes. Suddenly realizing this, Thomas added, "I'm sorry, horse. I didn't want to hurt you. I'm just frustrated, but I'm not frustrated with you."

Alderic chuckled at his friend's woe. "I'm sorry, my friend. We had grand plans of gallivanting the world. Perhaps we still can. You're focussed on what you're missing, but don't forget that your partner might feel the same. She likely had some plans too."

Thomas hung his head. "You're right. I keep thinking about this unknown girl as a thing, a masquerade partner, but I forget that she is a real person, too."

"That's understandable."

"No, but Father said not only is she sweet, but that she is smart, too. An intelligent girl probably had her own plans and dreams, too."

"You might be able to combine some of those dreams. Perhaps travel is an easy way."

"True." Thomas absently rubbed circles on the horse, which he enjoyed and relaxed completely for. "In fact," Thomas' face lit up, "We're supposed to be creating alliances between our people. It only makes sense to travel to each other's lands and explore the cultures, right?"

"Exactly. It's not all about marriage and babies."

Thomas grunted, brought back to the idea of marriage again.

"Everyone will be in your business, Thomas, but maybe taking a trip together gives you a buffer from everyone wanting to see an heir as soon as possible and lets you get to know each other authentically."

"Alderic, you're not wrong." Thomas sighed heavily. "I just wish it were different. Are you ready?"

"Yeah, let's saddle up."

The two men saddled the horses in preparation for training these two beautiful horses. Long ago, Thomas had realized that his father was right about this tradition, too. It had seemed utterly insane for a centaur to ride a horse. After all, he could shift into a strong, quick horse himself. But who better to train a horse than one who knew exactly what the horse was feeling? Indeed, the best trained horses were those from the centaur lands. Long ago too, Thomas had gotten over his sadness that these smaller horses could not shift like him. It was like some people having amazing hearing and some not.

Saddling the horses took a medium amount of time. They had worked with these two for several weeks and had them used to wearing the saddle, and even having weight on the saddle. Last week had been the first that they had climbed in the saddles and rode them around the ring. Today, they would bring them outside and along the trails.

The young centaurs led their horses outside, beside the outer ring that they had used yesterday. Both young horses dipped their heads to nibble on the sweet summer grass. Alderic and Thomas gently swung up into the saddles and let the horses shift and get used to their weight. Thomas' horse sidestepped a little nervously, but Thomas quickly soothed him with a firm hand against his neck and soothing words.

"Ready?" asked Alderic.

"As we'll ever be," replied Thomas.

So they lightly touched their heels against the horses' flanks and clicked their tongues as the horses had been trained meant to start walking. Uncertainly, the two horses began walking along the outside of the ring, used to following rails of some sort. Gently, Alderic and Thomas guided the reins to the left to lead the horses' heads away from the ring and towards the meadow. Skittish, the young horses danced sideways and then towards the taller green grass. Thomas and Alderic both patted the horses and praised them heavily all while keeping their voices calm and quiet.

They soon walked along the edge of the meadow beside the forest and then turned into a wide path (more a road, really). The horses began the trail easily enough, but soon became nervous as they were enclosed by the trees and forest noises surrounding them.

Chapter 3 - Aetherius

Most people attending the Quinquennial Masquerade Ball are young. In their teens and early twenties or the equivalent by their species. Demons age differently than some. Our lifespans, like fae, usually last for centuries. But recently it has been noted that our lifespans seem to be shortening or that the quality of life is dropping, just as the number of births is dropping. So this year, we are joining the alliances of the ball.

It is actually an interesting history lesson to search through all these species and see how some have interbred themselves almost out of existence. Others have been so warlike they killed off almost all their young men and had no one left to father babies, not to mention women who had been abandoned and felt just fine living without men anymore. But there are some species that it is unclear why they are fading. Why there are so few births each year? It really deserves further study to find the pattern. I think in those cases it is less societal, but perhaps cultural and likely environmental. In our case, it is quite easy to tell. About a thousand years ago, we became quite snotty. Removing ourselves from our own society to study. While studying, we did not marry, and we did not increase our population by much. Then, when several someones pointed out this would have long term negative effects, our hierarchy of fools decided that the nobility must fix it and we almost haughtily bred ourselves out of existence finding the purest and best breeding pairs. We desperately weakened our bloodlines and still have not recovered despite realizing our mistake several centuries too late.

It was funny, the reactions of some species that a demon wanted to join. I and several others had to explain that there are benevolent demons just as much as there are wicked angels. I am an eudaemon, and we are generally considered one of the "good demons". There was still a lot of skepticism about my right to be there. More so because it wasn't my parents arranging my partner to be. However, they had little to argue when I pointed out that I was older than their great, great, great, grandparents would be if they were alive and sitting at the table. I have lived through several of their wars and even ended a few of them. That actually, if what swayed the tide for me - actual evidence (once they raided the history books of the Great Library) of me being one of the "good guys," one of the protectors.

There were still some who couldn't quite swallow the idea of marrying off their precious daughter to a demon like me. They were moderately insulted when I told them that I wouldn't want the daughter of someone so uneducated or unwilling to learn. It left me with only a few options. The centaurs, the fae, and the vampires seemed most compatible. Quite an interesting group. Of those three, it is the vampires and the fae that live the longest, which would be potentially pleasurable in a mate. I lost the favor of the centaur when I explained that I did not need a mate to be by my side every century, but I did need to strengthen our interspecies relations and our bloodlines. Apparently, I'm unemotional.

I left the first meeting hopeful of the possibilities and reported back to my brethren. Another Eudaemon agreed to join the endeavor. This created quite a fuss at the second meeting, but I think we have it worked out now.

I look forward to meeting my bride-to-be. It really is unfair and ridiculous that they are not aware of who their mate is beforehand. Instead, there is this silly game to wear matching masks and find each other based upon cryptic clues. Something about finding worthy mates. But if it's preordained by these meetings, what would happen for those who do not find their mates, or make a mistake? Let's make no confusion; if we give cryptic clues and have both a gecko pairing and a lizard pairing or a tiger lily and a night lily, there are sure to be mistakes. Such silly games, a human must have designed it.

Chapter 4 - Brigid

"Guess what I received?"

"Noooo, you didn't, Brigid!?" exclaimed Sievonne.

"I did!" I held up my invitation. "For the Quinquennial Masquerade Ball!"

"Ohhh, I'm so jealous! We are going to make you look so beautiful!"

"Maybe you'll still get an invite." I suddenly felt badly. "Mine only just came late this morning."

"Perhaps, but I doubt it. My house does not rank as high as yours, don't forget."

"Hmmm. I would like for you to be there. What if I don't like my date?" We erupted in giggles together.

"I bet he'll be tall, dark and handsome. Or," she paused, "maybe blond and sun-bleached. Undeniably handsome, no matter what."

"Kind too," I added. "I would also prefer one who can carry a conversation. How do they pick the partners, I wonder?"

"I don't know. You should ask your mother. I'm sure the senator would know."

"Can you imagine being insufferably bored all night long at a ball? There is only dancing, music, and food. If you can't have a decent conversation, it would be horrible."

"You might have to talk about something other than books, you know."

"I can talk about more than books. Those books have taught me a great deal after all!" I got teased quite often for the amount I read, but truly, why did not everyone want to escape into stories and learn more about the world around them? I wasn't fickle. I enjoyed both realism and fiction, but what I liked most was discussing all that I had read."

"We must find you the perfect mask to make him want to chase you all through the evening and tear it off your face at midnight to kiss you."

She was so adventurous. "Could he not just slip it off my face and then we kiss?"

She threw a pillow at me, and then two more, and we erupted into another fit of giggles.

After a pause to regain ourselves, I asked, "Do you know anyone who attended the last Quinquennial Ball?"

My dearest friend, Sievonne, thought deeply then. She chewed the inside of her lip and then met my eyes. "I don't think I do. Between the fact that they are five years older and not that many are invited, I guess it makes sense, but it seems odd, doesn't it?"

"I thought so, too. I know we've heard of others going, but I don't think I have met a single one of them."

"Nooo." She pursed her lips. "You know what that means?"

I knew that look in her eyes. This was going to be a really awesome idea, or a very terrible one. "What?" I asked hesitantly.

"This means that we need to make you absolutely memorable. In five years, we don't want anyone wondering who represented the fae. Your dress, your mask, your jewelry, your royal escorts. It must all be stunning."

"Hmm. Maybe." There should be some sort of political twist we could spin on that for my mother's support. Something about supporting the common folk as they prepared my carriage, dress, etc. As a senator, she always wanted to be seen supporting the common people. I think she hoped they would feel we were one of them. But we didn't live in apartment buildings, or have to work fifty hours a week to pay our bills. We were descendents of the fae royals, as many were, and it showed. Our ears had that twist at the tip, we had that streak of white hair off our temple, and our teeth were just a little more feral.

"I think they instruct us about what our mask must be and then the dress and accessories match that. I wonder when we will learn that?"

"Oh, that's right, that's how the partners find each other, isn't it? You must find your matching masks?"

"I think so. Although I think there is also a riddle to solve. You're so much better at riddles. Now I need you all the more."

"Maybe if I don't get an invitation, I can be your lady-in-waiting."

"Sievonne! Your father would have a fit! You waiting on me!" I scoffed in disbelief, but she saw the truth in my eyes. I was excited about this ball, to meet some amazing man from another tribe. But I was scared too. It was a tremendous honor and therefore a huge possibility of dishonoring my family if I made a mistake. What if I couldn't figure out the riddle?

"Pfft," she blew off my concerns, "you read so much, you can probably figure out everyone's riddle and then decide how to twist them to get the perfect partner you want. What do you want?" She waggled her eyebrows at me. "Tall, dark and handsome or sun-bleached and smelling of summer grasses?"

For three days, I scoured our family library for every book I could find about the Quinquennial Ball. I even read a couple of novels about it. I'm sure they were only loosely based on the actual event. Those ended with some steamy scenes that had me both nervous and excited about the possibilities. Most of all, I was scared of not liking my partner. Whoever this partner was would eventually be my husband as well. It would help immensely if we could like each other, respect each other, and enjoy each other's company. I cannot imagine spending my life with someone who didn't love me, or worse, loved another instead.

I couldn't find that many resources that were factual, though. However, the librarian slipped me a note suggesting that there were more historical books about the ball at the House Lunaire's library. I actually know Brigittia Lunaire pretty well. We are the same age; we have studied together some along with a few other girls in the area. She loves books just as I do and we have had many fun conversations while our friends and cousins just rolled their eyes at us. Unlike me, she is also extensively trained to fight, whereas my mother thought a lady ought to learn skills like painting and sewing. I do like sketching, but the paint is awfully messy. We have done some trail riding together. Like everything else she does, she is a perfect equestrian. And she's gorgeous whether she is sitting studying, at a formal dinner, or sweaty and disheveled after a footrace. I used to be quite jealous of her. Then we became the best of friends over a book series. We seemed to be the only ones who read for pleasure and therefore had only each other to talk to about the books.

Anyway, I suppose I could send Brigittia a note to see if I might use her library. I would bet money that she already knows which books I'll want. I'll offer my resources too, despite their lack. But what if she didn't get an invitation, either? Will she be upset that I did? She's never struck me as the jealous type. I don't want to appear to be showing off. I just want more information. ...Hmmm. Dragon's breath, I just have to do it, I think.

Dear Brigittia,

I hope you're well. It's been a while since we have visited.

I am writing to you as a kindred spirit who loves books. I have been issued an invitation to the Quinquennial Masquerade Ball. I am absolutely delighted to attend, but as you might imagine, I want to know all about it beforehand so I can feel prepared. It turns out that our library is rather lacking in factual books despite a couple of novels with the ball included. I hoped firstly that your library might be better stocked and secondly that perhaps I could visit you to peruse the books. If you are interested, I am happy to bring these novels along for you to see.

Please let me know if you would be willing to entertain me. I have no idea if you have been invited too, (I hope so!), but if you have perhaps we can prepare together and share ideas for our dramatic outfits. I know we need to make a dramatic entrance to represent our fae people, but my darling friend, Sievonne, is more interested in making me frilly and beautiful.... I need your help.

I hope to hear from you soon!

Your friend, Brigid

Dearest Brigid,

Oh, congratulations on your invitation. I am sure you are excited! Probably more excited than I. I too have scoured our library for information. I have really found very little, but I'm happy to share. I can be free any afternoon for you, just send word ahead so I am available and not in the practise yard.

Excited to see you soon,

Brigittia

The next morning was one of those bright clear days that you itched to get everything done as soon as possible so you could just be outside and absorb the sun. Fates knew that the sun in the winter always seemed to be pale and in short supply. If only one could absorb this sunshine and save it.

Brigid had been daydreaming all morning about the Quinquennial Masquerade Ball. She was so excited to receive her riddle to figure out her partner. With the riddle would come the prompt for her mask as well. How perfect would it be if it were a wolf? She could copy her own pet wolf, Skye. Her mother, the Senator, had bought her the wolf from the Lunaire family. So she was excited to bring Skye with her as she came to visit Brigittia and her wolf, Zara.

Just as Brigid dismounted from her horse, Zara came tearing around the corner and gleefully attacked Skye. Skye enthusiastically bounced at Zara, and the two had a ferocious play brawl. Shortly, Brigittia jogged around the corner. "I was hoping it was you and Skye that so excited Zara," she laughed. Her hair was tied back, and she was in loose fitting training gear. "Sorry, I'm running late. I meant to be cleaned up before you got here."

"No worries," answered Brigid, eyeing Brigittia's outfit soaked with sweat.

"Uhhuh," nodded Brigittia with a knowing look. "C'mon, follow me up to my rooms and I'll rinse off and change so you're not faint with my poor smells and sweat."

Brigid walked along with Brigittia and the two wolves romped along behind them. Neither young lady worried about the wolves. They were known here and could always be found.

Brigittia called from behind the dressing screen, "So you're excited for the ball?"

Brigid broke into a huge smile. "Oh, I am! It's an honor to be chosen, you know."

"Uhhuh."

She doesn't sound quite as enthusiastic as I expected. "You must be thrilled, too?" asked Brigid.

"I am honored, yes, but there is quite a lot of politics involved." Brigittia hedged. She didn't want to hurt her friend's feelings, even if they weren't close friends.

"Yes, but the outfits and the food, and the dancing,-oh. That's not so much your thing, is it?"

"Not as much as yours, no."

Brigid watched her friend come around the screen, biting her lip like she was deciding something.

"Do you know how attendees are chosen?" asked Brigittia.

"Oh, I know it's about solidifying alliances between houses-"

"-Or species."

"Or species." Brigid wrinkled her nose a little at the thought of some species. "But they don't really match anyone who doesn't want to be matched, and even if they do, one night isn't a lifetime. Imagine being matched with a werewolf? Or a demon?"

"Or a vampire, that would suck," laughed Brigittia merrily and Brigid joined in at the pun.

After a moment, Brigittia asked, "I wonder how many of the dates from the ball stay together? Like, do they all get married?" She seemed very serious as she asked that.

"So this is why I'm here. I've been trying to research the balls, but our library has almost no information." Brigittia nodded as Brigid spoke. "In fact, all I could find were novels. In those, the couples all end up happily ever after."

"Hmm," said Brigittia thoughtfully. "It seems unlikely they would all marry happily, doesn't it? All these strangers with nothing in common."

"Yeah, maybe," Brigid answered, "I guess."

"Here, there wasn't much in our library either, but I grabbed these two history books yesterday. We can each read through one in the garden and compare notes. They seem to mention the balls."

Brigid felt immediate relief. Finally, facts, not just stories.

Chapter 5 - Brigittia

"You do have a scribe nature, Brigittia." Her ancient teacher spoke in a raspy voice.

"You taught me to be curious," she replied with a smile.

"Indeed, but remember, some doors are meant to be cracked open very stealthily and the contents are not to be spoken of."

"But we have spoken of the Quinquennial Masquerade Ball before."

"Very sparingly and very quietly," he agreed. "And we can carefully discuss it more, you and I."

"But no one else, I know," Brigittia pulled a face.

"Not even your young cousin, whom I expect, is quite excited at your prospects."

"I know, and she is. And I can't lie - we already know this - so she doesn't understand why I'm not trembling with anticipation and burning with excitement."

"Indeed." He nodded sagely. "What do you wish to know about it, in particular, that we may find the best texts to help?"

"I don't know...actually I don't know what I want to know, but I want to know all that I can about it. I want to be prepared for every possibility."

"So you are preparing just as you would for a battle?"

"I," she paused, considering, "I guess I am going into this thinking of it like a battle. It is all about power, and intentions, and the higher ground. However, I have hope to make the best of it as well. It dictates direction for the rest of my life. I would like to steer my course a little."

"Right then, Little One, let's take a look." He thumbed his lip pensively. "I think you could bring your grandmother's journal to your room and no one will think twice about it. So let's find that and tuck it in your pocket for later.-

"-my grandmother was at the ball?"

"Indeed. She was far too smart to write about the politics of it, but I expect that she wrote about some traditions and customs. It may help you a little to read about the ceremony and routines from when she was your age. There will be differences, but my, how people like tradition."

Wide eyed, Brigittia nodded. She had never considered that her grandmother or even her mother might have been one of the attendees of a previous ball. Too bad the dear woman had died when Brigittia was still a very young girl.

She followed her tutor between the stacks of books and scrolls until he paused. "This is the history section I think we may find of most use. Ahh yes, here is *History Common Between the Lands* and *Politics Between Species*. You start with these two while I look for some older ones." He handed her two old leather books.

After an hour of straining against poor handwriting, Brigittia rubbed the bride of her nose and then her temples, hoping to stave off a headache. She could really use some cafe right now, but there was no way to have that in the library. She could at least enjoy a cup while reading her grandmother's journals. That handwriting was much larger and less spider webby. It was a darker and clearer ink too. Though given time, it would probably fade as these had.

Just then, her old tutor appeared with three more books. One of which was bound in green leather, of all things.

"Slow going, this reading, isn't it?" It was a statement more than a question.

"Ugh. The handwriting is so difficult, not the reading itself, just reading the words."

"Aye, it's a strain on the eyes. But here, I've marked the pertinent parts of this text for you. Are you done with these two?"

"*Politics Between the Species* reads like a report written by my little brother. It is vague and assumes that one already knows what is being spoken about. Written about, whatever."

The older man snorted with amusement. "The other one, *Common History,* is more helpful, but harder to read as the ink is more faded."

"Perhaps that one we take with us and resume after a cup of cafe. Not," he wagged a finger, "with a cup, but after a cup."

"That would help," she agreed. "Can we take these others you just brought?"

"We could, but let's see if they are worth carrying with us first. This one here, I told you I marked the passage, is quick. Read it while I look closer at these."

Brigittia opened to where the ribbon marked a spot and scowled in frustration.

"What?" asked her tutor, just a little too innocently.

"It's written in old Elvish."

"Why, so it is. It will be good practice for you." He chuckled and then added, "but it is only about three pages, so it won't take you long."

"Ugh." But she blew a strand of auburn hair out of her face and plopped her chin in her hands as she studied the text. She could read Elvish, both the common and the old, but it took concentration. Two paragraphs in, she sat up. "Wait, three hundred years ago they realized they were breeding themselves out of existence?!"

"So it seems."

"How old are the Quinquennial Masquerade Balls?"

"Not that old at all. In fact, I believe the next one is the Centennial Ball."

"So what did they do for the two hundred years before that?"

"Keep reading."

Brigittia grumbled, but kept reading. "Oh. Clearly. They went to war to rape and pillage and spread their seed. How did that work for them?"

"Keep reading."

"Oh."

"Indeed, 'oh'. They discovered they were half right. Spreading their seed seemed to create stronger, healthier babies than what their perfectly royal marriages had wrought. But going to war had killed off nearly all their strong young men. There was no one left to continue spreading their seed nor young warriors left to protect their homes and families. The older warriors did their best to protect and farm the lands, but it wasn't the right solution, either."

"No, but we need to give them credit. They are introspective and learn from their errors."

"Correct. And they were observant enough to realize that other species were also dwindling."

That must have been quite an interesting meeting when they first sent out diplomats to broach this problem in other kingdoms."

"Indeed. And a lot of wine."

Brigittia couldn't help it. She giggled. "Truth."

"Help me wrap these and we'll bring these back to the study." The old man carefully wrapped the green leather book in a soft cloth and tucked it into his bag, while Brigittia wrapped the other two. Then he slipped them into his bag as well. Together they walked out of the silent library and into the bright afternoon sun, blinking at the harsh light.

Cafe did indeed help her headache as did the jelly pastries, or at least they helped Brigittia's mood. Continuing through the spidery, faded ink was still frustrating, but it grew more interesting as she went. Zara, Brigittia's gray wolf, lay contentedly by her feet watching or anyone coming near. Occasionally her ears twitched, but all afternoon remained quiet. With half a mind, Brigittia considered whether she could create a matching costume for Zara and bring her to ward off unsavory characters. More than likely, other ball goers would misunderstand Zara and assume she was a threat when she wasn't. She could be, but it wasn't her everyday nature to be threatening.

Brigittia found that all the books wrote endlessly of the benefits of the ball, and only one mentioned any negative ramifications. She marked that one to come back to it. Consistently, it seemed, the political allies cemented through marriage had staved off numerous wars and some other skirmishes. A couple countries had apparently merged under one reign due to their marriages, as well. At least twice, Houses who were almost mortal enemies with each other married, and it was only then that the fighting between them stopped and the warriors could stay home and procreate. Some of these foolish Houses had nearly wiped themselves out until someone started sending heirs to the balls.

It also seemed that some bloodlines were more sought after than others. Vampires were seldom sought, but the fae almost always were. Silly, it seemed to Brigittia - an alliance with the vampires would be far harder to achieve in normal years than alliances with fae Houses. She wondered what sort of price her marriage earned. Since she couldn't know her partner until the ball, Brigittia had no idea whether she was sought after for her babies or her House name.

Starting to slip into a "why me" and "it's not fair" mood again as she thought about her personal dreams, she refocussed herself. She decided to look into the dagger question that her cousin had brought up. Were weapons really not allowed, or was it just expected that they couldn't be brought? And were the same expectations in place for men and women? Because if she couldn't bring her blades, she should practice with some of her other weapons that could be hidden in her combs, belts, and jewelry. She was willing to bet she wouldn't be the only high lady with a small blade hidden in her shoe, either.

Then there was a surprise in the *Politics Between Species* book. Apparently, about 70 years ago, there were several suspicious deaths *at* the ball. The evidence clearly suggested poison. A poison that caused the person to suddenly choke and not be able to breathe. This turned their face beet red or maybe purple. They were clawing at their throat, one attendee ripping their shirt off and causing quite a scandal. Then the people would pass out, foaming at the mouth, and their face continued to swell. It appeared to be a terrible way to die. At least three people died from this poisoning and there was another death that was very, very similar. The historical account was unclear whether they were in fact poisoned and just reacted differently, or if they died for some other reason.

There was huge fallout from these deaths. Multiple Houses accused other Houses. Per the norm, it was the werewolves and the vampires that were accused the most. It wasn't until the Archangels stepped in that violence within the Ball itself was curtailed. Two of the dead were actually a pair to be married. The other two deaths almost caused more wars as their mates were left unmarried. Feuds between Houses continued and escalated into the next years. The following year, those "widows" were re invited, but rumor had it, according to the history book, that they were unwanted and considered unlucky. While they were married at the next ball, they both dead within five years. One reportedly died of suicide, the other maybe died of heartbreak. The recording historian seemed sympathetic, but unsure.

However, most balls seemed to be quite scripted and political. Either alliances were formed affording more secure borders or alliances were made to strengthen bloodlines. There seemed to be scripted events within a strict order of events that all the ball attendees were required to complete. Every single ball was described as extremely opulent and over the top. Whichever House hosted, they wanted to host the best and most unimpressive ball ever.

Chapter 6 - Thomas

"I don't understand," said Thomas.

"I feel like this is our constant mantra these days," sighed Councilor Victor Briarthorne.

"But Dad-"

"No, I know. It's my fault. Just forget I said anything."

"I can't just forget it. You said you learned who my partner is at the casino."

"Right. I wanted to tell you now in case there was a crazy rumor later."

"Ok, I get that, but you're not actually telling me anything."

"No, I guess I'm not."

"And you won't tell me who my partner is for the ball?"

"No, I'm sure you'll be able to solve the riddle on your own. We both know you can't lie at all, and it would be odd for you to walk straight to your partner."

"Hmph." But Thomas couldn't argue with his father's logic. He could not carry the farce that he didn't know something. "Fine. So you found out before you were supposed to and you want me to understand that. Ok. That's why you're sure already that she's a nice person?"

"Right. I have had time to get to know her family. I actually know her mother from my time on the Council. Her mother is...ruthless when she believes she is right. I think her daughter is as strong willed. She is just as intelligent. Like you, I believe she loves to read."

"So at least we may find some books in common to talk about that night." Thomas actually felt better with that kernel of truth. He didn't particularly like small-talk. So talking about books, even ones he hadn't read, would be far easier than just conversational drivel.

27

"I just don't want you to hear something and fear the gossip mongers who twist everything about."

It seemed odd that his father was so concerned, but Thomas knew his father well enough to know that he would get no further information out of him at this time.

"Ok, I guess I just do my thing and ignore the gossip. You know, like normal."

Councilor Briarthorne chuckled and gave Thomas a tired smile. "Exactly, my son. Thank you."

Thomas wrinkled his brow, but just said, "Sure. If that's it, I'm going out to the barns."

"Go ahead, my son. Thank you." *The rumors will catch up to him eventually that I won his partner in a poker game. She is a nice girl, though, even if her mother isn't.*

"I dunno, Alderic, he was being strange."

"What do you mean?"

Thomas pondered it for a minute, while using handfuls of straw to rub down the horse following today's workout. "I mean, it's weird, yeah. He hasn't bothered to talk to me about rumors since I was just entering school. So, why now? Why is he concerned about me hearing rumors now? What's different about this rumor?"

"Hmm. Your Da rarely worries too much about you hearing rumors. They're always on about how he voted, or will vote, or some ridiculous story of something he supposedly did. You've known not to believe the rumors for a long time."

"Right."

"So, what are you thinking?"

"I dunno. But it feels like he is trying to get ahead of it. Like maybe there's something true being covered up in the rumor, like it's partly true."

"Truth is stranger than fiction, yeah?"

"I guess. Or maybe there is something more shady than just that he learned about my partner too early. Like maybe he got to choose her or something."

"That would be a big deal. And even bigger if he told you."

"Which he won't do."

"Sure, but how do ya prove that?"

"Right." Thomas rubbed his own forehead with the straw, then shook his head to get the dust off his face away from his eyes. "I mean, anyone who knows me knows I can't tell a lie, but most people who might care about this sort of thing won't know me at all."

"This sounds like a right pickle. Hope ye don't even hafta worry about it."

"Yeah. I tend to worry, and then things aren't even an issue."

"Right. And is your worrying about it helping at all?"

"Well,... no."

"Right. So finish rubbing down your prince there and let's move onto the next two colts."

Thomas knew his friend was right. So he finished rubbing down the horse, gently tugged a tangle out of the mane, and gave a soft tap on the nose. "See you tomorrow, Prince." Then he stepped out, carefully closing the stall door behind himself. Alderic was right, there was nothing he could do about rumors or reactions to rumors now. He could, however, work with the next colt to teach him not to be afraid of his own reflection every time they passed a puddle.

The envelope sat on his table. Thomas was filled with anticipation and trepidation. He was sure it was the riddle, the clue, to who his date should be. His mother would be thrilled because once read, he would know what his outfit should be influenced by and his mask could be designed.

But Thomas was nervous. *Riddles are tricky. What if I make a mistake? What if I can't figure it out? What if everyone else figures out theirs, but I can't and my poor date is wandering alone? Will she just run*

away because I can't decipher it? Of course, she's supposed to figure it out
too, but they're supposed to be tricky. What if I make a mistake?

True, the ball was only one night, but usually the couples ended
up sealing alliances between houses and actually getting married.
Whoever his partner was, he wanted to find her right away and impress
her. He wanted her to solve hers right away too, so that they were
equals.

He picked up the thick envelope and then set it down again. *This is*
ridiculous, he said to himself.

Thomas wiped his hands on his pants and then picked up the
envelope again. It had a distinct smell; he realized. Unfamiliar and
familiar all at once. Like cinnamon and sandalwood and oranges and
...something.

He slipped his thumbnail under the seal and gently tried to open
the envelope. His thumb was too calloused and rough, and the heavy
cream paper ripped instead. Grimacing, he carefully tore it open
further.

Greeting sir Briarthorne,

Congratulations on your invitation to the Quinquennial
Masquerade Ball. House Everhart is excited to welcome you to our
lands. We do have a few requests to keep everyone as comfortable as
possible:

Please arrive with no more than one carriage, one driver, and one
attendant if needed. Thomas snorted. He did not intend to bring
anyone with him. *Although, come to think of it, was he supposed to drive*
his date home at the end of the evening? Maybe he should bring a driver
and carriage.

Please arrive no more than an hour before the start of the ball at
7pm and please arrive promptly with no tardiness.

While you may bring a drink of choice with you, we shall have
plenty of options of food and drink and will not have any servants

available to "jaunt out" to your carriage to fetch your supplies. *What exactly had happened, to require this stipulation?* Thomas wondered.

You must wear your mask as soon as you may be seen by anyone other than your own staff (including our footmen). You must remain wearing your mask through the entire ball.

No weapons may be carried into the ball. *Carried, huh? There were ways to work around that.* He would certainly feel more confident with at least one blade and a rope. For the ball, a cord might work.

Once entered, you must stay until the closing ceremonies. You will be directed when you may leave.

Please take care of your riddle. We do not want any down crest emotions to dampen our event.

Sincerely,

House Everhart

The second sheet fell to the floor, and Thomas quickly dropped to one knee to grab it.

Clue #1

I roam the world with a mighty roar,

Fierce as I explore.

King of the Wild, with moonlight grace,

My royal presence, you can't erase.

Your color choices are important and must incorporate red and black. Silver is your metal.

What the heck, this could be anything. Well, anything large and predatory. A dragon roams the world and is fierce. But a lion is considered the king of beasts. Lions aren't out in the moonlight, are they? Maybe. Just because we think of them sleeping in the sun doesn't mean they don't hunt at night. Actually, just 'cause they're graceful doesn't mean anything about being in the moonlight. Again, that royal presence. What other animals are royal? If we think about the king's signet then it's a falcon, which are graceful and fierce, but I don't think of them as a nighttime bird, or even

King of the Wild, but if they are the king's bird I guess that makes them King of the Wild.

Thomas crumpled up and threw the riddle across the room. Then he hastily snatched it back up and smoothed it out. He hated this stupid ball more and more.

Thomas did not much care what he wore to the ball, except that he be comfortable, played to his strengths (good shoulders, for example), and not bring shame to his house. He would, of course, have a small hidden blade in his belt, and the chains around his neck could be a weapon in a pinch.

However, I should make time to meet with the tailor, he grumbled to himself, *or he'll dress me in some concoction of a cross between a butterfly and a bear.* He snorted to himself then picturing that. *What a popular match I would be!*

Regretfully, he pulled on clothes that were easy to slip on and off and walked to the tailor's shop instead of going for a run in the fields. The sun was still low, and the warmth of the morning was comfortable, not hot like it was likely to be later. *Why couldn't they make the stupid ball in the winter when there aren't a million things to do outside? Or make it fun for young people with a bonfire or something. The middle of summer is the perfect time to spend an evening outside!*

The bell above the door tinkled with a cheery alert and the tailor waved him in. He didn't say anything at first, as he had a mouthful of pins. This was not at all unusual, so Thomas took a moment to really look at the fabrics on display. There actually were some interesting fabrics that seemed to shimmer in the light between dark, blood red at one glance to black emptiness in another. Would blood red be unlucky, or was this almost black the perfect choice?

Thomas jumped when the tailor spoke behind him. "That is an interesting fabric, isn't it, old boy? Sorry, sorry, didn't mean to make you jump. I thought you heard me walk up." After a moment's pause and Thomas' saying 'no bother', the tailor continued, "I don't think I have ever seen you pay attention to a fabric before it was sewn."

"No, but this time the colors matter, don't they, Sir Shadowstitch?"

"Indeed, lad, they do." He rubbed his thumb, a habit Thomas had noticed before when the tailor was thinking. "I would love to work with this fabric, quite challenging, but then a stunning finale from it. However, for the ball, that is what you're here for, right? Yes, for the ball, do you think it may be too dark? Or just right? Hmm?"

"I, well, I um... Choosing fabric isn't really my thing. I just let you do it normally. Or my mother." Thomas hesitated a moment, but then rushed on, "But I do really like this fabric. It's like it calls to me."

"Ohh," the tailor slowly smiled. "Good, if it calls to you, especially since you've never felt this before, then this is the one you must have."

Thomas furrowed his brow in confusion, but before he could ask, the tailor urged him onwards towards the side window.

"Come then, over here in the light. Let me see how we'll drape this on you. Umhmm, yes, it does fit you."

He draped it over one shoulder and then around Thomas's chest, murmuring all the while. Then he rolled it back up to drape it again over Thomas's shoulder all the way to the floor. He stepped back then. "Ummhmm. Good, I love how she subtly dances in the light. Turn to your left please, no, the other left. Yes, yes, this is definitely it. Wait until you see it with a mirror, but it almost looks like you are wrapped in burning embers, like you are holding the wrath and power of fire within you. Oh yes, this will be a masterpiece."

Thomas couldn't quite see it the same way, but he had a hint of the idea as it flared out a little as he turned. It looked like fire and coals trailing beside him.

"Oh yes, that is a masterpiece. We'll need very careful measurements, lad, so we can do this perfectly. This is not your standard black suit. Hmm, what about the mask?"

"The mask?" Thomas rapidly blinked his eyes, trying to catch up.

"Yes, yes, the mask. Will it be this material too, or would you like a contrasting color? Or a silver wrought mask with this underneath to peek through and be comfortable against your face?"

Thomas had never answered so many questions about his own fashion.

"I um, I uh...I think whatever you think best, Sir Shadowstich. You are the expert here. I'm afraid I'm out of my depth."

They both chuckled at the truth in his words.

"Well, yes, but at least you have the sense to come see me. We'll make it right, and," he waggled his eyebrows suggestively, "we'll make all the girls want you."

Thomas blushed dark red, almost matching the crimson in the fabric.

Thomas leaned against the wooden fence, arms up on the rail and right leg stretched as far behind him on the ground as he could. His goal was to stretch his hamstrings as much as he could. His ragged breathing slowed as he switched legs. Just as he rolled his head from side to side to ease the tension in his neck, he glimpsed movement beside him.

"Rough morning?" asked Alderic

"Ugh," sighed Thomas. "I hate going to the tailor's because I don't actually care about fashion, so I can't make the right choices. Then I hate being groped and measured as if I were a show pony. I'm surprised he doesn't pull back my lip and count my teeth while he's at it."

"You do have all your teeth, don't you?" Alderic asked, mock seriously. "I have to confirm that before accepting your official invitation to the ball."

Thomas mock angrily pretended to punch him and they both laughed.

"Seriously though, I would rather do any kind of hot and sweaty, nasty dirty work than deal with that."

"You did it though, old boy. Good job. And then I see you came for a de-stressing run."

"Well, it was that or strangle the old bloke, and I didn't think that was a good choice. So I came for the run that I wanted to do instead this morning."

"I see. Very mature of you," snickered Alderic.

"Shut up."

"I'm only half joking."

"I know. That's what makes it worse."

Alderic held up his hands in surrender, and they began walking.

"You know what else I was thinking about last night?" asked Thomas.

"I hope it was about some pretty girl, but your voice leads me to think otherwise."

"No. Well, maybe, hopefully, but not exactly."

"Huh?"

"Yeah, so I was thinking, I'm pretty sure that a lot of these couples get married. At least we've heard of a bunch of them getting married. What if my alliance is to be married off to some far-off kingdom?"

"Doesn't the girl usually go to the guy's lands?"

"Yeah, usually. But usually people get to pick their own partners in life too."

"You're just a ray of sunshine, aren't you? Look, maybe she's beastly or a cow or who knows what. But maybe she's amazing. Maybe you'll just become best friends and this alliance doesn't have to be a marriage, but a partnership in business or a peace pact. Who would force you to get married if you didn't like each other? Sure, there was a time in history that we did that, but not now. That's ridiculous."

Thomas grunted.

"You sound less than impressed. Did anyone say you're meeting your bride? DId your dad say this will be your marriage partner?"

"No, and no."

"So stop worrying about nothing."

"Yeah, I know. But this is nuts and driving me nuts."

"You need a drink. And I'm not afraid to go with you, just to keep you company."

As Alderic expected, Thomas laughed, and soon they were headed back to Thomas' rooms to change and then find their way to the local pub. Some frothy, ice cold, grainy, hoppy, beers foaming up glasses would be the perfect way to spend the rest of the afternoon. Thomas hadn't really accomplished much that day, but all his horses were progressing nicely in their training and he could slack off once in a while. At least, that is what he planned to tell his father if he was asked.

They stepped through the door of the pub, and a little bell jangled. The barkeep looked up and smiled warmly. "Ahh, must be a peaceful day at the stables, hey lads?"

"Right, Maeve, or we just decided we needed your sweet company."

"Flirting is free, Alderic, but ye still pay for yer drinks."

Thomas smiled watching his best friend flirt with Maeve. They had known her forever, before she ever became the best barkeep around. They had plenty of secrets they had shared, from hiding her away from her abusive family for days at a time, to stealing kisses in the library.

Maeve narrowed her eyes at Thomas seeing his anxiety and began pouring him his favorite beer, a strong, almost yellow one. Then she turned to Alderic, who never could keep a favorite for more than a month. "What'll it be, Alderic?"

"Surprise me, lass. No, on second thought, don't. I didn't like that last one."

"Come now, that was supposed to put hair on yer chest, and the molasses sweetens it."

"Have you tried it?"

"I'm not an idiot, no."

They all laughed some more. The bell over the door welcomed another patron, and Maeve stepped away to help them. In a moment, she was back.

"Alright, Alderic, have ye made up yer mind?"

"I dunno. Pour me one of the ones I have liked in the past. The more hops, the better."

"Right-o. So what has yer hair in a knot?" She looked right at Thomas as she asked, "Yer worried or anxious about something. Do ye have a sick foal?"

"Nah, it's nothing so serious."

"No?"

"No, it's the stupid, Quinquennial Ball, and I'm all out of sorts anxious about it."

"Ohhh, ye were one of the invited ones?" She turned to Alderic, "but ye weren't?"

They both nodded, and she continued. "I always dreamed of going to that when I was younger. All the gorgeous clothes, the music, the food. So many species to interact with right up close. Ye may be anxious, but I'm a wee jealous."

"I would trade places if I could," offered Thomas.

"Aye, ye would too. Ye've always given away all ye have, but I think yer date might be rather disappointed expecting a strapping young man, and instead getting big bosomed me."

"I like those big bosoms!" said Alderic.

She whipped her towel at him. "Quit yer droolin'."

"But when you show them off like that, right out in the open like—"

"Get off, ye lout," but she laughed as she scolded him, completely unfazed by his staring.

Chapter 7 - Aetherius

As I expected, this ridiculous riddle is vague and could be many things. The colors and the metal help. It must be the humans figured out that there needed to be extra clues for each pair. Still, I've seen a couple of these riddles now, and they are laughable.

I have some unique abilities, including an ability to listen from afar, so I should be able to listen in on my partner and see if she figures it out. If so, good, she is an intelligent girl. If not, I'll figure out how to nudge her along.

Meanwhile, we are two months before the Quinquennial Masquerade Ball, and I still have my regular duties to do. Here's the thing with demons, both greater and lesser. Lord Lucifer, while technically in charge, doesn't really care what most of us do. Most of the demons are running about, causing issues among the worlds and stirring up anger, jealousy, and pain. These all feed into a weird energy vortex which actually fuels the levels of Hell. Some of the angst converts to gemstones like rubies, some of it - the anger I believe- converts to energy that we use for electricity to power our lights and such. Some of it trickles into some form that actually fuels Lord Lucifer himself. This is why he is most powerful during seasons that the species are filled with lust and hate, not the seasons of love and complacency. Most demons tend to stir up the former and not the latter, so he gives them a light reign.

Then there is us, the good demons. Ask a mortal and there is no such thing as a good demon. Ask a fae and they say, I think my grandmother mentioned white demons once. Ask a vampire and they say "of course". Vampires are actually quite similar to demons, both far more powerful and so misunderstood by society at large. Either can be killed, but it is so difficult that we are considered immortal.

So us good demons are sent to police the wicked demons, or to counter influence the lesser species. Ever hear of someone doing something wrong for the right reasons? More than likely, one of my brethren was involved.

I'm off to do some watching today. Unlike many demons, I like to take my time and make sure I understand the reasons someone is making their choices. Are they truly greedy or are they stealing to help someone else? Are they lost or just desperate?

For example, as much as every species would like to ignore the homeless in our communities, we all have them. I watched an old man in a homeless camp for a few days. He was incorrigible, going out every day and stealing. He would slip into the employee bathrooms of stores and steal everything out of their first aid kits. He would steal food from anywhere he could find it and bottled drinks, too. He even stole balls out of strollers he passed. I mean, stealing from babies is the lowest of low, right?

I followed him, this grubby old man who always had a kind word for people. He wore a long coat and had a lump on his shoulder that really made him look like the hunchback of Notre Dame. I watched him and saw him slip off the coat when no one was watching and saw the disfigurement was actually the bag he kept his stolen goods in. I saw him move items from it into his huge coat pockets. Then, as he shambled along, I watched him hand out first aid supplies and snacks for the parents of children. I watched him hand over bottled drinks to the women, too sick to move from their boxes. Someone else seemed to supply them with meals from the church. I was following him through camp when suddenly we were swarmed by dogs. And then those stolen balls reappeared. He must have spent an hour throwing balls for those dogs, their homeless owners cackling with delight to see their pets having such fun.

At the end of the day, he sat down by a fire that a young lad lit for
him, and ate an apple and a granola bar. I realized it was the first time
that I had seen him eat all day. He drank from a plastic bottle that was
dirty and creased, with no remnants of the original label. He must have
refilled it through the day at the bathrooms he stopped in at.

I sat down with him, asking to warm my fingers by his fire. I shared
a sandwich with him. Delving into his memories, I saw he loved grilled
cheese with tomato, and that's what I just had in my pocket. Not warm
and gooey, but grilled to that perfect golden brown. His eyes lit up at
the simple pleasure. I spoke with him for hours. We talked about how
he didn't mind camping outside. It reminded him of being a boy scout,
but he worried for the young families and the older feeble members of
his community. Eventually, I used my powers to affect him. I seldom
do this. I hate to interfere with emotions, but I knew he wouldn't just
accept help, even if it was for the greater good of his people. Of course
he was wrong to steal, but he did it to help those children and parents,
those unable to care for themselves, and those dogs dependent upon
others who were struggling themselves. So now, every week, a case of
various first aid supplies appears in his tent (I upgraded him from a
box) along with chew toys and even some cat toys. Cats are better at
keeping down the mice population. There is a crate just outside of view
of the common passer-byers. This crate is where he now deposits some
of the items he steals, but it is always filled. Refilled as if by magic. He
goes days at a time now without stealing, but rather restocks from the
crate and delivers the items around camp to those in need. Others help
themselves.

Really, how hard is it to help people? Why punish him for stealing
when he was doing it to help others?

Standing tall in front of the mirror, Aetherius let his onyx-black
wings elegantly unfurl behind him, adorned with ethereal patterns that
caught the subtle light. His obsidian eyes, though intense, held a depth
of kindness and understanding as he considered that he would be

meeting his bride tonight and likely she had never intended to befriend let alone marry a demon. Few fae would. Few mortals would. Most mortals feared demons and, with good reason, his brethren had not been kind. Ironically, his partner would be among the safest being on earth. No other demon would dare to anger an Eudaemon.

If only they could all see, we are the good demons, those who right wrongs. But we are also vengeful for any who try to harm those we seek to protect. No one will harm my bride.

He studied his complexion - a blend of midnight hues, flawless, and a subtle loneliness. The fae would not be used to darker skin tones like his. She dealt well with a variety of people and species, but demons were never wanted. Perhaps he should use a glamor for the start of the night and let it slowly fade as she got to know him. He shook back his raven-black hair, and it fell off his shoulders in silky waves, framing a face that seamlessly combined allure and benevolence. A well-tailored black ensemble with under colors of deep violet and midnight blue accentuated his perfectly sculpted body. Small silver owls were embroidered on his collar and his cuffs. Larger and more intricate owls were embroidered on his upper arms. His mask, once he put it on, was shaped to look like a large horned owl. The mask was primarily black but with iridescent purples and blues woven in just like his real feathers upon his wings caught and twisted the light.

Contrary to the tales of demonic mischief, Aetherius's smile carries a touch of melancholic wisdom. He is a demon not of malevolence but of complexity, a being whose beauty is matched only by the compassion that resides within his enigmatic soul. In the celestial tapestry of existence, Aetherius stands as a testament that appearances can be deceiving, and even demons can possess a captivating nobility.

He sucked in air through his teeth, considering, and then pulled on a faint glamor. Adding some tones of yellow and warmth, he softened the darkness of his skin to a more mortal color. He would bank on her being too polite to ask his species type at first. It really was a shame that there was all this secrecy around the ball. They could save time and stress by exchanging letters first or even meeting before the ball, and it would make that important night all the easier. But mortals, especially humans and their fallacies, thought this was so much more exciting. Or maybe the ones in charge feared a rebellion against species like his and thus gave the attendees no choices to back out.

Still, he had left some books about and he saw that she had found them, and even another, interesting that she could read old Elvish. At least his partner had an inkling that the ball would lead to marriage.

Since she knew that, better that he not scare her at first with his odd appearance. He could leave the wings out, he thought. She seemed to gracefully accept all varieties of species. She would probably be inquisitive about them at first and it might be a way to increase their physical contact right at first. The more he could mix their auras, the quicker she might relax and she subconsciously get to know him.

He exhaled deeply and began putting on his various leather bracelets. He seldom wore any metal jewelry, hence all the silver trim on his clothes, and tonight was no different.

Chapter 8 - Brigittia

My grandmother's diary was a treasure trove of information about my entire family. I started skimming through to find entries just about the Quinquennial Masquerade Ball, but soon found my attention captivated by her descriptions of daily life. I could hear her voice through the writing, and it was as if we were sitting together in the garden as she dished out the gossip and the news, interspersed with advice and opinions. Her diary was just an extension of her. I swear I felt her love enveloping me as I read it, too.

It made me wonder why she had written all of this down. Did she expect someday for someone like me to read it and learn from it, or was she simply unburdening her mind of it all - clearing her thoughts for the next day? I don't know, but it was a treasure trove. I'm sorry to say it, but this I will not share with Brigid.

My grandmother was very good at mixing super important information right in the middle of fluff, seemingly talking about one thing while clearly describing something else to anyone with brains enough to read between the lines. It took me a little while, but I soon figured out that many of the pets she wrote about, and their antics, were actually the doings of houses, defined by their animal sigils. Oh, she was a sly one. When I did realize what she was doing, I wanted to slap myself for being so blind. I had been so confused about why a raven hung out so often with a boar.

Last night I had just gotten to the part of her talking about receiving her riddle. Apparently, that was the year that they added a themed metal as well. Previously there had been just an animal riddle and color suggestions, but some struggled to find their partners for hours. Adding a third clue into each clue would help.

Like me, my grandmother had blue, black, and silver. She had chosen to rebel as much as she could by wearing just black and silver with hardly any blue. She wore blue, but only a miniscule amount. I may do the same. Unfortunately, there won't be the blood rubies dripping down my cleavage like my cousin, Titania, wanted. Maybe I can work blue sapphires into tears. Black seems fitting for a funeral, which this ball is to my youth and freedom. The girls like Brigid are in for a shock. She thinks she is only to be partnered for this dance and then go on her merry way if she likes. I know that we are to be together much longer depending on our House's needs.

I went to bed last night before I read my grandmother's description of the actual ball. I wanted to be fresh for that. The way she weaves so much truth into what sounds like frivol, I'm going to have to reread it several times, but I wanted to be fresh for the first read. But, the anxiety in me is ramping up, and I had crazy dreams. I was running into the fancy ball and tripping over everything while searching for my partner. In another dream I was so terrified of making a mistake and then this angel came and wrapped me in his wings until I calmed again. Then he led me on his arm to the front of the crowd and demanded silence while I looked at everyone in quiet until I found my partner. Another time, all the ball attendees turned into the animals that their masks represented and it was a wild rumpus ending when the prey were being ravaged and eaten by the predators. Suddenly everyone regained their humanlike forms and women were fallen everywhere in ripped and bloodied white dresses. That one is pretty easy to assume was innocence being torn away from us. The partygoers turned animals seems to make enough sense too, but the angel who comforted me...that I don't understand. Why would an angel even care about our ball, let alone little old me? Angels and demons don't really interact with us.

I hurried through my daily chores and my weekly correspondences so I could sit and read my grandmother's diary. I wouldn't dare take notes. Her secrets would be safe with me, but I did want to concentrate and remember every detail possible.

Finally, I sat down on my balcony overlooking our private gardens. Other rooms look down on the ornate flower beds. Mine is a little different. First there is a landing pad of grass for Zara because she leaps to and from my balcony. Then there are beds arranged around that patch spiraling out with herbs and flowers used in our kitchens and our infirmary. I love the medley of scents as these grow and later when they are harvested. There are also beds of my favorite flowers that I may pick for my room or for the halls I walk through the most. Lastly, right below my balcony are blackberry bushes that I care for quite carefully. The berries burst with flavor on your tongue and quickly stain your fingers. But the thorns are not quite deadly, but try to climb through them and you wish you were. They are defiantly aggressive with long thorns that curve, branches that bend and bounce and are tangled in such a way that you cannot climb through. I believe it's good to guard my space.

Now I am sitting here, stretched out on a lounging chair, with a cafe beside me and a blackberry muffin. I pick the berries for the kitchen and they use some to make me muffins. The sun feels glorious on my face, and I take a moment to close my eyes and let it sink into my skin. I want this feeling to last, but I have a feeling that once I continue reading my grandmother's journal, the warmth in my spirit will disappear. Zara decides I will not share my muffin with her and she snuffles at my face. Then turns sticking her head over the railing.

"Go ahead, my girl." She turns her head to look at me, then steps back, bunches her legs, and sails over the railing to land on her patch of grass. She holds her nose to the breeze, her ears twitching, then trots off. She'll be back when she is ready.

I sigh and pick up the journal from the cushion beside me. But before I open it, I take a sip of cafe and break off a chunk of the muffin. Popping it in my mouth, I settle back to be comfortable while reading.

The ball was all I thought it would be, and so much more. I had figured out my riddle before the ball; I was pretty sure, but there was still a niggle of doubt in my belly, making me nervous. But I loved my outfit, and I was confident I represented our house well. My riddle was a hummingbird. My colors were to be blue, silver and black. Boots are easiest in black, so I chose boots that were comfortable even though they had high heels. Fancy and practical.

My dress was mostly black lace with silver gilding trim. The under colors were vibrant sapphire blue. As I moved and the dress spread and waved, the lace would open like the outer feathers of a wing and the underlayer of blue shines through. It's gorgeous, it meets the requirements, but it also resembles a dress for a funeral. I look like I am all in black as I stand still. The funeral of my youth and freedom.

My mask is mostly silver and blue with teal and greens shining as well. All the beauty of a hummingbird is in my mask and my jewelry. In case my date is a dull bloke, I have a hummingbird in silver and blue that wraps around my ear that looks as if it is alive and resting there. The silversmith outdid herself. The craftsmanship (craftswomanship?) is amazing.

This creates me to be a hummingbird with more sapphires dripping down my face to encircle my neck and then trickle down my back and front into my cleavage. The sapphires draw the eyes to my best features, but also represent my tears. There is no obvious show of revolt, but my resigned emotions are demonstrated with elegance. The magic imbued in the mask could hardly be felt, but brushed my face as gently as hummingbird feathers.

Magic? This I wanted to know more about. But infuriatingly, Grandmother skipped past it.

It turns out my date was the perfect accompaniment to me. He found me almost immediately, and leaned down to whisper in my ear, "My tailor forced me to wear predominantly blue with hints of black. What I envisioned was what you have. You are gorgeous and we have much to talk about." I'll not lie, not here at least. My heart did flutter at his words. It seemed, from his tone, that his emotions matched mine and that gave me hope.

He led me to a table that he had already claimed. "I like this vantage to view the entire ball from." Indeed, we could see almost everywhere in the room, "but I don't want you to feel ostracized. Show me a friend of yours and I'll invite she and her partner over to our table so you have comfort."

"And will you have a friend here, too?"

"I would like to."

"That's fair." I genuinely smiled for the first time in what felt like weeks. He smiled back, and I knew then that we understand each other quite well.

Chapter 9 - Brigid

She had spent an amazing afternoon with Brigittia. It was hard to say who was more tired when they finally arrived home that evening, whether it was she or Skye. Skye had romped with Zara in their wolfish pleasures for hours. She and Brigittitia had spent hours reading through old history books, more had been delivered to them, and taking notes.

Their notes had been very similar. Brigittia seemed less surprised that there were such numerous inter-species couples. Brigid had always believed that most of the couples were just between Houses and very few between species.

"I had no idea there was so much of this!" Brigid exclaimed after the fifth reference that she had found.

"We do need to consider how many couples are at each ball." Brigittia was good at keeping to facts and reason. None of it seemed to surprise her.

"True."

"I think, from reading through these, that the balls used to be much larger. But none of these except one have numbers listed. Nonetheless, the historian mentioned that because of the plagues that year, the ball was smaller than normal with only 75 couples."

"Do you know how many couples will be there this year?"

"No, but I wonder if we can ask our parents to find out how many attended five years ago. Surely there must be records they could access. It's an innocent sort of question."

"Of course it's innocent," said Brigid puzzled.

"We may know that, but don't forget that everyone will be watching all of us who attend, and other ball attendees watching you too, and they love to suggest that your accidental sneeze was actually a secret signal."

"Damn." Brigid's face fell. "I forgot, I guess, how deeply the politics will be ingrained. Everything we do will be second guessed, won't it?"

"Uhhuh. Everything we do or don't do. Everyone we talk to. Anything we wear or carry, or don't wear or don't carry."

"Yeah," Brigid answered softly. She had been dumb to forget this basic lesson. She knew better.

"Speaking of which - no blades can be carried in, but you have weapons you can wear, don't you? Just in case?" asked Brigittia gently.

"You mean like a boot knife? I have one somewhere."

"Wear it. But no, not just that. Do you have any that can be disguised as a brooch or a hairpin? Something?"

"Hmm. I'll have to see." She paused. "Actually, I'm not completely bereft. I have a hand fan that hides a blade. I will find that and see if I can work it into my outfit."

"Yes! Or have another made if you are more comfortable with that than a blade in your hair."

Brigid nodded.

"Seriously. You should have something else just in case, but it needs to be something that you can actually use relatively easily."

"Yeah, no, I know. I don't practice with blades like you do. But I should go a few times before the ball. Make sure I can draw and hold it correctly, at least."

"Uhhuh, you should be confident with it. But...?"

"But?" Brigittia sat silently while Brigid thought. "Oh! I should practice, but not let anyone see me practicing. No need to give them more to talk about."

"That's right. They'll talk no matter what. Make sure they talk about what you want, like your gorgeous hair." Brigittia smoothly moved the conversation to topics more comfortable. She had planted the seed; time to let it rest.

"Oh, yes!" Brigid's somber face lit up. "I have so many ideas about how to put up my hair and weave in jewels, but until I know what my mask will look like, I can't decide."

"You could just design a gorgeous mask in your house colors and then use the riddle, when we get it, to design your dress. That way, you can start to choose your hairstyle and jewelry."

"Oh," Brigid bit her lip, "but most people will have masks with their animals, won't they?"

"Sure, most of them. But this could be one thing that you choose to have them talk about. Something that you don't seem to care what they think, that you'll just do you."

"Hmm, that is sort of freeing, isn't it?"

Second seed planted.

Greeting Lady Vale,

Congratulations on your invitation to the Quinquennial Masquerade Ball. House Everhart is excited to welcome you to our lands. We do have a few requests to keep everyone as comfortable as possible:

Please arrive with no more than one carriage, one driver, and one attendant if needed.

Please arrive no more than an hour before the start of the ball and please arrive promptly with no tardiness.

While you may bring a drink of choice with you, we shall have plenty of options of food and drink and will not have any servants available to "jaunt out" to your carriage to fetch your supplies.

You must wear your mask as soon as you may be seen by anyone other than your own staff (including our footmen). You must remain wearing your mask through the entire ball.

No weapons may be carried into the ball.

Once entered, you must stay until the closing ceremonies. You will be directed when you may leave.

Please take care of your riddle. We do not want any down crest emotions to dampen our event.

Sincerely,

House Everhart

Brigid squealed with excitement as she read her official invitation and her riddle. She was disappointed that one of her colors was black, but how fun it could be to match with Brigittia who also had black as a color. She pondered the riddle. The moonlight king had to be a wolf, wasn't it?

King of the Wild, with moonlight grace,

My royal presence, you can't erase.

She could imagine a tiara with moons and stars if it was to show off royal presence. A silver lacy mask with stars and moons along the edge would be far prettier than looking like a dog. Maybe black satin under the silver for her own comfort. She did not think that metal against her face for hours would be very comfortable.

Now to design the dress. This will be fun! It would be easy to incorporate fur into the trim, but that would be awfully hot for a ball. So how do I symbolize an animal in a beautiful dress?

I wonder if my partner loves wolves too, or if that is entirely for my benefit? If we could both love wolves, it would be auspicious for how well our friendship could grow. And if he could be a reader, too...

Brigid spent the next days sketching dresses and masks, then sharing them with her best friend, Sievonne. After they had found a few designs they liked, she sent them off to the seamstress and silversmith.

"You're sure it's a wolf, Brigid?" asked Sievonne.

"Why, of course, what else could it be?"

"No, well, I thought...no, maybe you're right."

"Why? What did you think it might mean?"

"King of the Wild is usually a lion, isn't it?"

"What?"

"Didn't it say 'King of the Wild'?"

"Well, yes, but it said 'moonlight grace' so it would be king of the night, wouldn't it? That would be the wolf."

"Hmm, yes, that makes sense."

"But you're not convinced, Sievonne?"

"I, well, no. Not entirely. And red suggests a lion more than a wolf, doesn't it?"

"Why, blood could be from either."

"Umm, well yes, but red is royal and usually associated with lions, not wolves. Wolves are blues and silvers, and well, darker."

"They are both powerful. They are both silent and fierce...unless they are not."

"True."

"But you still think that I'm wrong."

"I want you to be right when you walk through the doors, whether it's a wolf, a lion, or something else."

"Ok, yes." Brigid bit her lip. Sievonne was right, of course. She needed to be sure. "Let's look at it some more. But the mask we could still go forward with. We need to use silver, and clearly the relevance of moonlight is there no matter what."

"Yes, I think that we can indeed use nighttime symbols on the mask. And then incorporate the animal into your hairpieces and the dress. We have some more time to be sure."

"That's smart."

"Let's go for a ride. It will clear our minds."

"Yes, being outside always helps us think. You're right."

"Or perhaps a game. That always helps with my frustrations, too."

"Skuash?"

"Oh, yes! Perfect!"

A few minutes later, the ladies were dressed in sporting clothes and out against the garden wall, passing a ball between them by battling it against the wall with their racquets.

Brigid swung hard, but missed the ball by only the slightest breath of air.

"Your miss, my serve," Sievonne chirped.

"Indeed," agreed Brigid, smiling grimly.

But the next three volleys were all Brigid's win.

Both ladies were hot and breathing hard. "Pause?" asked Brigid.

"Oh thank the Goddess, yes! I need water."

"Right. Maybe something else but plain water."

"With mint added?"

"Or wine."

"Oh!"

Chapter 10 - Quinquennial Masquerade Ball

The Everhart House had gone all out preparing to host the Quinquennial Masquerade Ball. As carriages rolled through the gate and up the drive, guests could see gorgeous landscaping highlighted by many characters holding lanterns to add to the full moonlight.

As each carriage pulled up to the steps, plenty of House Everhart staff were available to aid anyone out of their carriage, and if needed, whisk them to a hidden room to freshen up. The carriage was ushered to a spotless rear yard to unhitch the horses to let them relax in open airy stalls with fresh water and a little hay provided. Likewise, there was a common area for the drivers to relax and moderately drink and eat.

Once the guest was ready, they were led up the steps by a handsome footman to the grand hall. All around, and yet not in the way, were decorations. Most were tall tree-like plants that had been formed to look like partygoers. There were also flowing garlands of flowers, ribbons, and blown up decorations. Everywhere there were bright feathers and masks of every shape and size. Tall flutes of light champagne and wine were served. Those who arrived a little early could mix in the hall, but promptly at 7pm the huge oak doors were swept open and guests were invited into the Ballroom.

Upon walking through the heavy doors, one immediately felt like they were translocated to a different world. At the far end of the room, and it was an enormous room, was a magical fireplace. It was like a standard stone fireplace, open in the front and large enough to roast an ox, but filled with flames that were blues, pinks, purples, scarlets, and oranges. There was a faint scent of cinnamon and cherry wood in the air, as a little smoke wafted into the air - not enough to irritate the eyes or nose, but just to give an underlying scent.

Candle sconces with similar flames were scattered around the walls, but most of the light came from a sky scene above that seemed to be thousands of shining stars. The light this way was soft, steady and plentiful, but not too bright. Scattered around the room, twinkling lights designed to look like fairies and butterflies were draped over tree branches in darker corners of the room.

There were multiple tables scattered around the room with little cups of fresh fruit and berries. More glasses of sweet wines and champagne were available, too. In other scattered locations were barrels of ale and beer, tapped and ready to be poured by House Everhart staff. There were tables set for dining and seats for eight to twelve, depending on the size of the table. Each place was set with simple glass plates and gold silverware. Napkins of gold and purple were set across the plate and tied with miniature masks. Tall glasses were at each place, with pitchers of ice water available. Each table had a different centerpiece but without fail, they were low enough to see over and included fresh flowers. They also were interwoven with tiny masks and ribbons of purple and gold.

Every guest paused to gape for a moment as they walked in. Then a House Everhart staff motioned them forward to find the table map to see what table they were assigned to start at. Traditionally, guests were mixed together to meet new people, but with no relation to their fated match. This allowed for a variety of conversations before dinner and for new friendships to be forged. Oftentimes, it also allowed for quick alliances as one tried to find their match, or last-minute riddle solving. It was not expected that most guests would find their partners until after dinner, and dinner was served not long after the guests arrived.

The more cynical of guests assumed that this was so the guests could have something to do, eat, while the hosting House bored them with welcome speeches and went over the rules. Much to the surprise of some guests, there were many rules given to them, which helped preserve the traditions and the secrets of the Quinquennial Masquerade Ball.

Chapter 11 - Brigittia

I took a deep breath as the carriage pulled up to the steps. It was real. I was here at the Quinquennial Masquerade Ball. A rather cute House Everhart footman opened the carriage door and offered me assistance to climb out. I put my hand on his arm to be polite, but easily stepped out and down the folding step. Music floated out of the house to greet me, along with fabulous ball decorations. Nervously, I adjusted the mask on my face. I was under strict instructions to keep it in place until we were told to remove them at midnight. I immediately regretted that sign of nervousness and vowed not to repeat it.

I took another deep breath through my nose. He was kind enough to pretend not to notice, and then he led me up the grand stairs. Heady perfumes assaulted me from the many flowers used to decorate with, and mirrors accentuated the bright lights in the hall, almost blinding us where we gathered. Someone handed me a glass of champagne. I wanted to gulp it down, but made myself sip it. I could not afford to get drunk or even tipsy. I had to be on my top game.

I looked around and tried to recognize somebody to speak with and to calm my nerves with. At first, it was just overwhelming, with garish masks and huge gowns. But after a moment, I began to see past the masks and see the faces under them. I imagined others were seeing me the same way.

Also like me, I assumed that they were all carrying a weapon of some sort in their fancy clothes, and that they had magical wards somehow on their bodies. We might be on a hundred blind dates, but we were also used to protecting ourselves from potential dangers. Especially in a group of uneasy alliances. It was ironic that blind dates were somehow supposed to solidify alliances and make us safer. I gigged as I realized this, and suddenly there was a chuckle beside me.

A man laughed softly at me. I spun to look at him. Tall, dark, and handsome. Literally, he was in all black with just hints of dark violet and stunning blue. My eyes widened slightly at his black wings curling around his shoulders.

"I'm sorry, I shouldn't have laughed at you," he apologized quietly. "I just couldn't help but notice how frivolous this all seems, and then here you are, looking around and chuckling at this madness."

"Yes, well," I stammered, "I don't mean to be rude, but I did laugh. I was thinking that we all have some sort of blade and magic on us to keep us safe from each other, as these alliances between houses and species are...tenuous. And yet, we're using a hundred blind dates to somehow solidify those alliances. It seems a bit preposterous."

He chuckled again. "It does, doesn't it? I agree. And yet, here we are."

I was interrupted from answering as trumpets blared and the great doors to the ballroom swung open.

Lights and music poured out of that great room, along with tantalizing scents of food. I almost wanted to eat because it smelled so good, but my belly was still tight with nerves. I knew I was safe. I had a half dozen weapons on me that I was an expert with and I could even hold off grown men my size or a little larger. Moreover, I had magic wards sewn into all my clothes and drawn on my body with invisible ink. There were also the ones tattooed on my body from when I was only a week old. The lines were still as sharp now, nearly two decades later. But there was just so much secrecy about this ball and what happened at it. I took another slow, quiet breath through my nose. I would show no weakness.

"Shall we?" asked the winged stranger as he held out an arm to me.

I hesitated, not sure whether I should take his arm. I needed to find my date after all, but ultimately decided that we could enter together.

I slipped my arm through his and we joined the line to enter. If others thought I had already found my partner, then they wouldn't be looking as hard at me, thereby allowing me to watch them more easily. Ugh, I already had a tension headache forming. But, I felt oddly comforted, because this very composed looking man beside me had a tremor pass through him when I took his arm. He was extraordinarily tense as we walked in, even though he kept his face calm.

It took only a moment before we were at the head of the line. Turned out that everyone was being paired up with someone close by, so no one would find us an odd pair. There was an usher at the door, making sure there were exactly eleven seconds between couples entering. I have no idea why eleven seconds, but we heard him clearly counting it.

"Ten, eleven, walk forward, please."

We walked into an elegant room, decorated so extravagantly and yet so elegantly. I had never seen anything so beautiful and so garish in all my life. The smell of roast ox was stronger now, but it was mixed with fresh flowers, savory herbs, wine, and a heady incense. It was hardly yet crowded, allowing me to quickly see all the guests. We found a place to stand off to the side of the giant fireplace and watch the rest enter.

Guests slowly scattered and found their tables. I didn't recognize anyone at my table, but I kept catching the eye of the black-winged fellow I walked in with. Why did he keep watching me? I couldn't help it. I touched my mask to see if it had fused onto my face crookedly. I didn't think so, and besides, what could I do about it?

I feel a little bad that I had slapped my friend Ellern. I just couldn't get her to calm herself and I didn't have time for hysterical drama. It did the trick. She pulled herself together. Now she's at a table behind me, fairly close, and I can sometimes hear her voice charming and friendly as she maintains conversation. If I didn't know her as well, I would think her fairly composed. But I can still hear the lacy edge of panic in her voice. She's doing well to mask it, but I know her. I vow to myself not to give way to my own emotions.

So I chat with those at my table. There's a faun named Gilbert, but Gilly for short. A few fae from houses that I have heard from, but never met, and they seem to be best buddies and uninterested in the rest of us. There's a vampyre named Steve. I wonder if it's really Stephon, but I won't ask him yet. There's a lupine shifter named Maeve, a satyr named Steve also (who planned that?) and a fellow whose lineage I can't put a finger on. His name is Leon. Other than the two fae, everyone at my table is courteous and considerate. We chuckle a little at our discomfort and quickly find commonality.

The first Steve, the vampyre, thinks he has spotted his date across the room. Indeed, there is a gorgeous woman staring at him and when he catches her eye, she lifts an eyebrow and smiles at him. When he shares his riddle, we agree that his winged bat matches her dark robe "wings". The other Steve mentions that his riddle was distinctly under the sea themed and he dreads meeting a mermaid. So we point out every sea creature, including an octopus, that we see.

Suddenly, the world narrows to the view of only the most gorgeous man I have ever seen. He is stunning. He has walked over to speak with Gilly, the faun, but my ears are ringing and all my senses are on fire. I'm drawn to him with every fiber of my being, except maybe my brain.

"Brigittia, did you hear me?" The words finally penetrate.

"What?" I blink crazily, and my owl costume must look complete this way. He has wings, and a mask that shows a beak as well. Is this stunning, muscular, tanned blond man my partner? He's clearly a bird.

Gilly laughed, "You're doing it again, Thomas, stealing the girls, and she's not even my date." Then he turned to me, "I said, this is my friend Thomas. Our families have been friends for years."

I dip my head in greeting, feeling a stray feather tickle my ear, "Pleased to meet you, Thomas. I'm sorry I was distracted for a moment."

"Oh, that's alright, Br-Brigittia," he hesitated over my name. "No worries, it's a little overstimulating here."

"Right," laughed Gilly. "And the way you two are staring at each other like love struck teenagers. Hey!" He snapped his fingers between us.

We really were staring at each other. I wondered if he was a siren - the pull was so strong.

"Are you a siren?" He surprised me by asking.

"No!" I laughed nervously. "But I was just wondering that about you."

Gilly looked back and forth between us. "What did I just miss?"

The hairs on my arm stood up then, and one of the sigils on my back tingled. Someone was directing magic at me. I dropped my napkin on the floor and used picking it up as a pretense to look around to see if I could tell who was focussed on me.

Chapter 12 - Brigid

B rigid had been filled with nervous excitement the past few days. She had hardly slept the night before. In fact, she spent time laying down today with ice under her eyes, to smooth the bags away. She took a little nap also so she would be bright and cheery all night long. She needed to have all her wits about her to make sure she found the right partner, her partner. But she also needed her wits about her to be a worthy partner and achieve the goals that her House needed from this blind date.

Brigid stood in front of the mirror and slipped the silver mask onto her face. She had tried on the dress and mask a week before. Then, the black satin under the mask was stark against her pale face. Tonight, her face was rosy with pink hued excitement. The makeup around her eyes was bright and showed off her golden brown eyes. The white streak of hair that sprang from her temple was coiled back and tucked behind her ear highlighting the slightly pointy tip, while the rest of her dark hair spilled down her back and framed her face in heavy curls.

Her dress was silver, with threads of purple and black woven in. It looked much like the fur of her wolf, Skye. Her silver mask looked like fine lace and covered half her face, then lifted up with what looked like a canine ear. She absolutely was representing as a wolf. She could completely explain how her riddle meant this. But there was still a niggle of doubt.

Her nerves were at an all-time high when her carriage pulled up, and she needed a few extra breaths before standing up to climb out.

"Are you ready, m'lady?" asked the footman courteously. He had given her a moment to catch her breath, but he would have to have her carriage move if she needed more time. There were more carriages behind and he couldn't have a delay.

"Yes," she took a wavering breath, but met his eye. He could see her stubborn determination. She stood up and stepped out pretending confidence. He could feel her tremble, but he didn't break her act and stood solid as she stepped down. Like several other ladies, he simply held out his arm and walked her up the stairs. They both knew he was ready to catch her if she fainted, but he simply looked polite. He was very good at his role.

"Thank you," she whispered as they reached the top of the stairs.

"Good luck, m'lady," he nodded and stepped away and returned to his post.

Brigid stepped into the hall, heavy with the scent of flowers and decorated with so many streamers and masks that she couldn't find a single empty surface. Someone handed her a glass of champagne. She took it, but she asked the waiter for a glass of water. She sipped at the champagne until she saw him coming back. Once he made eye contact with her, she swallowed the rest of the champagne, then when he handed her the water, she poured it into the flute and handed back the glass. She would keep sipping that. Hopefully, the champagne was enough to give her some liquid courage for a while.

Brigid moved forward to the heavy doors that opened to the grand room. Amazing smells and music spilled out. The people in the hallway moved forward steadily and if they were not already paired with someone, they were given a random partner to walk in with. No one walked in alone, and there was a regular pause between every pair. This kept the movement steady, but also kept the guests more comfortable. Nobody had to enter alone and face a stare-down gauntlet.

"Ten, eleven, please walk forward," the sentry at the door directed them to move forward.

Brigid and the man dressed in yellow and black. He resembled a bumblebee with a golden torque at his neck, but she smiled and they moved forward. At first, the room was completely overwhelming with the scent of roasting meat and flowers and heavy incense, plus people everywhere. As soon as she could politely, Brigid moved away from the stranger and back towards a large tree-like floral display. With that at her back, she could scan the room and get her bearings. She quickly located a sign with table assignments posted. She would make her way over there soon. About all that would tell her was who her partner wasn't. They were never assigned seats at the same tables. She sipped her water and scanned the room again. She didn't see another wolf, but that was ok, many people hadn't arrived yet.

Chapter 13 - Thomas

The footman opens my door and waits for me to step out. There's no fanfare or anything, and I'm quite grateful. I arrived in the middle of the rush, hoping that I wouldn't be very noticeable that way. He is nice enough to give me a quick check when I ask him if my mask is on straight. Even a quick word of encouragement, "You got this man. I hope you get one of the pretty ones."

"Thanks," *I think.*

I climb the steps, taking a deep breath, and plaster a polite smile on my face. I have a ruff around my neck. The designer says it could work as a falcon or a lion, a little safety buffer for me. But the damn thing tickles my neck and face. Swatting the little fringe away, I scan the crowd in the hall for another lion or falcon. There were crazy looking birds, some sort of fish, and many other animals, but I don't see lions or falcons. Soon enough, I find myself paired up with a unicorn or something and we were ushered into the great hall. The heady incense tickled my nose even more than the ruff and I sneezed for three minutes straight.

Before long, the hosts stood in front of the giant fireplace.

"Thank you guests. We welcome you to our home." A portly gentleman spoke loudly and the crowd quickly quieted. "There are one hundred guests here tonight, fifty blind dates, if you will. You are all welcome and you are all safe since you all left your weapons at home, or in your carriages." He chuckled knowingly. "A few of you will get your weapons back when you leave.

Now, there are a few rules about the Quinquennial Ball you may not know. First, I think you all know that you may not leave until dawn, when you are released. By your faces, I think actually very few of you knew that. Alright, I'm sorry if you thought you were leaving shortly after midnight. It will be dawn. There is a certain romance to riding off into the dawn, right?

Second, you will have seen the board beside me here. This has your seating arrangements for dinner. Your blind date is not assigned to your table. This allows you to eat in peace, with no need to impress anyone, but also fosters a chance for you to meet new allies for your houses. There have been many strong friendships forged at tables like these.

Third, you have been instructed to leave your mask on all night. This is nonnegotiable, even if you step out on the balconies for fresh air." He smiled gently and continued, "Please take a moment to adjust your mask so that it is most comfortable. It will be attached to your face for many hours. I'll wait." Everyone adjusted their masks slightly while surreptitiously looking to see if anyone moved their mask enough to reveal their identity.

A sudden gust of wind came through and stirred up the heady incense. Several people sneezed and everyone's eyes watered. Never had incense been quite so strong. Then there was a tingle that moved from their watering eyes to their cheeks, and a heat spread across their face. Not only a few tried to wipe under their mask. Gasps filled the room, and then a few screams and a lot of swearing.

The man who had been speaking cleared his throat and then spoke loudly above the noise, "Ladies and Gentleman, tied to rule number three, your masks are now fused to your faces and will remain until the spell breaks at midnight. Since I'm sure you are now so completely distracted, I'll let you recover from your shock, search for your partners, and find your seats. Enjoy your evening. I will speak more with you later." With that, he walked away, and the crowd really didn't notice.

I quickly found my table, but for my sanity, I also sought out one of my dear friends, Gilly. He is a faun, so we enjoy many of the same things, but we come from very different Houses. My father has no interest at all in politics, unlike Thomas' father, the councilman.

I walk over to Gilly without hesitation to say hello. But mid-word, I am captivated by the beauty beside him. She clearly is a bird too, with her beaked mask and feathers in her crown. We have similar colors and silver. My heart jumped before my brain realized all of this, but clearly we are drawn to each other. So much so that the words slip from my mouth before I realize, "Are you a siren?"

She blushes and stammers, "No, but I was just wondering that about you."

It's fate, clearly, that we so quickly found each other. Or maybe more of this strange magic we are subjected to.

Suddenly, she breaks the spell as she looks down to pick up her napkin. It's like this squeezing in my chest loosens. I breathe again.

Gilly looks between us, "What did I just miss?"

"I,I,I don't know. Is there more magic being used upon us?"

"Oh, most definitely," mumbled this beauty, dressed as a bird in blue and black.

"What happens then when the magic wears off?" I asked.

"That depends upon the intentions, now doesn't it?" She flashed me a smile, but from the glint in her eye, she seemed not to be thinking about love, like I was.

There was a trumpet blast then and servers began carrying enormous platters of food, and we stragglers were ushered to our tables. I hurried to my seat, but I made a request from my table mate and switched seats so I could keep my eyes on her. She was regal and gorgeous, and calm. She, too, switched places, so she could see me more easily. Even without speaking, we seemed to think alike.

The first course was delectable with salad or soup. I chose salad as I always do. The greens were crisp, and the variety was good. Most of my tablemates chose the soup, and they seemed equally happy. There was good brown bread served too, a mini loaf for each of us, and salted butter on the table.

While we were finishing these first dishes, a variety of appetizer-like foods were set on the table. There were rolls of veggies seasoned and grilled, chicken wings of some sort, some kind of dip with sliced vegetables and breadsticks. There were mini grilled cheese sandwiches and cups of sauces and a variety of seasoning and salsas.

A few people moved between tables when they recognized a friend or thought they might have found a partner. But for the most part, we followed instructions and stayed at our tables, getting to know the people there. My tablemates were nice, and I found commonalities with all of them, but I couldn't fully concentrate and found myself just staring at her. Soon enough, my tablemates were teasing me a little about her. But not too badly, actually. They agreed she was gorgeous, too.

The main dish was served then. Some people had chosen some sort of fish meal, but I had a beef dish. The scents when it was set in front of me immediately made my mouth water. I don't like fish at all, but even that smelled decent enough. There was plenty of alcohol served, too. I could see that beauty drinking all through the meal, but unlike some at her table, she didn't seem to be losing her poise. I wondered if she was like me, alternating between water and alcohol. The beer was cold and frothy and I would have loved to have sat back, stuffing my face with this delicious meal and just swigging back the beer. But it's not that kind of night. We should all be on our toes and alert for all the political alliances or un-alliances, truthfully. I hate this stuff.

She keeps her eyes moving over the crowd, but gives attention to everyone at her table, and I bet she could tell you their whole backstory and a lot about each of their Houses, too. Nor does she seem to care about what species anyone is. Constantly observing and judging worth, but not like most people.

There's a lot of people looking around the room, and a number of people notice her. I see one guy boldly walk up to her and try to slip her something. She kindly takes it, but later I see it crumpled and dropped on the floor, then she kicks it under the table.

Chapter 14 - Aetherius

Hmm, turns out there was a surprise for me too. I didn't know our masks would fuse to our faces. There are a few of us who are not panicking. More than likely, those who have realized the masks cannot damage us, or after every ball, there would be a tremendous commotion. Indeed, almost anything done with magic can also be undone.

So, I guess this tradition forces the partygoers to actually talk to each other and not unveil too early. But I confess I'm not sure why that is necessary. Too much a part of my mind is puzzling that and I forget to pay attention to the guests for a moment. It actually doesn't matter much as most of them are freaking out and tugging at their masks or frightfully fainting. It bears noting who *isn't* doing that. These are the more intelligent and the unintelligent. It is the middle of the pack that I fear the most. My eyes find my date, who apparently hasn't recognized me as hers yet. She is the one standing calmly and crowd watching. Our eyes meet, and her eyes are as calm as her body. Good then, not an act. Although she has been trained as a warrior and would carry herself as unafraid, even if she was terrified. But the calmness that radiates from her is soothing to some of those around her. I nod my respect at her, and she gives me a tight smile back.

She shocks me then as she yanks up the woman next to her and slaps her. I focus more of my attention on her so I can hear her words, "Stand up, Ellern! This behavior is beneath you. Obviously, what has been done with the masks will be undone. Else we would have heard of it from every person who attended these balls in the past." Tight logic there. But whether it is the logic, the slap, or just a familiar face, albeit masked, the hysterical woman is calming. I look forward to having her in my court. I need someone who can calm a crowd, and clearly she has the presence needed.

There are other pockets of calm spreading, but there are definitely still areas of hysteria. I see servants from the house coming around with more wine, and persistently offering them to those who are hysterical. Also not a poor plan. The incense smell changes as well and now is less heady and more...lavender? Something calming and soothing. Hints of lemon, and maybe mint.

It takes about thirty minutes before calm returns across the floor, although the ranges of emotion are quite amusing. Some people are clearly frightened. Some are very angry. A few fools have gotten completely drunk, and I sincerely hope they are partnered with each other and not causing any problems for others. As the calm returns, I see the Head of House returning to the room. At some point, he must have decided he can claim the audience's attention again.

"I'm sorry everyone, that was quite a rude surprise, wasn't it? Quite shocking, I imagine, quite shocking indeed. But I can assure you, as some of you have said, that all previous Quinquennial Ball guests have had this experience and are none the worse for wear. You, too, will keep the secret for future attendees."

Interesting that he says that we will. It implies that there is no choice, no free will.

"So now, if you have not already, it is time to find your assigned tables and make friends with those who are seated with you. Those at your tables are not your fated partner. They can and should be your allies. If you already know your partner, you could recognize the other octopus at first glance, for example,-" the crowd laughed appreciatively as the octopi waved on cue. "If you already know your partner, we encourage you to help your tablemates find their partners, enjoy the meal, and then spend the next few hours getting to know each other. You and your partner were paired for some reason, and seldom do the pairs not succeed.

"So go forth, find your table, look about for your partner, and enjoy the meal. There are only a few more surprises planned tonight."

With those ominous words, he again left the room. The idea of surprises does not comfort me. I see my mate's forehead is furrowed with concern as well.

Suddenly, a young lady crashes into my chair, clutches it, really. She holds herself well, but I quickly see she is in shock, but not from the crazy announcements. No, I realize as she stares at her wrist that she just received her fated mate's brand. Apparently, he's the blond hunk who was just talking to my mate. Interesting that we haven't received our brand yet. I know who she is, but she hasn't recognized me as her mate yet. I calm this lady for a moment and then offer to walk her to her seat, passing right next to the boy, of course. One more set of partners figured out won't be bad, and once he sees he is her fated mate, it will be a less distraction from the girl he was macking on. My girl.

We walk together towards Mr. Hot Stuff. I can feel their bond pulling her, but he doesn't seem to even notice her.

"What's your name, dear?" *If I can introduce them, then maybe I can push them together, right?*

"What? Oh, I'm Brigid." What the Hades. These girls are so similar, even their names are almost identical. No wonder the lad is confused. I wonder if Brigittia's nearness confuses his bond?

"Brigid, what a lovely name. You know, your costume reminds me of a lupine or leonine animal."

"Really? Yes, yes, I'm a wolf, but I'm not positive that is right. The riddle was difficult."

He groaned. He couldn't help it. "These damned riddles. Why not just tell us our dates?"

"Right?! It's so stressful!"

"Hmm, and your mate, he has pointed ears and-"

Then, because surely we had been enjoying the calm for about ten minutes, the room was plunged into darkness. The shrieks were dreadful! However, this darling girl who had struggled behind my chair hardly faltered. Her fingers momentarily gripped tighter, but she didn't jump or shriek. She remained calm and just stopped moving. Honestly, my instincts were either to run for cover or stop short and observe, so it worked fine for us.

When the lights blinked back on, we had all been shifted to the sides of the room, tables whisked away and a dance floor appeared. Apparently, we were done with dinner. *How had they moved me without me even feeling it?* This was powerful magic indeed. Being a demon, albeit not a fallen angel, I expect my magic to be some of the strongest in the room and yet I didn't even feel a whisper of what just happened.

We look around, reorienting ourselves. I quickly find my mate, but hers takes a little longer. "Here, let me walk you over to him."

"No, wait, he's not dressed like a wolf."

Damnit, no he's not. What the Hades.

"Hmm, that ruff around his neck is like a wolf's ruff, no?"

"I think I'll watch him, but there must be someone dressed here as a wolf. Tonight is just one night and alliances. He'll be around later as my mate."

I open my mouth to answer and am completely shocked for the second time in a minute. I literally cannot answer her. I cannot force the words out of my mouth. I try again. And fail again. So I try something different, "Observing him can't be bad. But," again my voice freezes on what I want to say.

"But?" she queries, finally looking at me again.

"But don't wait too long. Grab him if he is the one."

"Yeah. But someone may be staring at me like I'm looking at him."

"Uhhuh." *I really hate half humans.* "I think you need to be proactive and look out for yourself and your House. Be the wolf."

"I am a wolf." She mutters it, but I hear it. "I am Skye."

"You're the sky?"

"Sorry, I didn't mean to say that out loud." She blushed an adorable shade of scarlet and involuntarily stepped back, as if to hide. I stood still and calm, and she quickly recovered. "I said that I am like Skye, my pet wolf."

"Ahh, that explains the mask, the wolf. I see why you would think that to be your answer then. My mate also has a pet wolf. Apparently, it is far more common than I thought. Be the wolf, Brigid, and seize your mate. Do what you need to in order to best represent your House."

"Then I better be sure not to embarrass my House. I'll keep looking."

Grrrrrrr. "Better to take action than be left behind."

"Uhhuh."

Meanwhile, I have been looking for Brigittia, but I haven't been able to see her. At least the boy isn't macking on her right now. I see other birds, but no other owls, so she should be able to figure this out easily. These stupid riddles. So while I'm looking, I try again to speak my mind freely about the ending expectations of the ball. Again, I find the words frozen in my throat. I stop then to avoid looking like a bubbling fish. Apparently, I cannot warn her.

The music starts playing softly then and dancing seems imminent. Our Host steps to the middle of the dance floor.

"Come, let us dance and be merry. If you have found your partners, by all means spend the rest of the evening in their company and get to know them better. If you haven't found your partner, I urge you to swoop among partners until you meet. Now, my lovely wife will come forward and we'll start the dancing. Please come join us!" The music began to swell louder until she had walked out and held his hand. Then they began a sweet waltz. After a minute, other couples began to join them. It was mostly the outrageously obvious disguises that came out, the octopi, bears, unicorns, and jellyfish to start with. Then a few others tentatively began to dance, and these were not all obviously paired.

I narrowed my hearing at a few of them, but there was nothing very interesting being spoken. Much complaining and a lot of confusion.

Chapter 15 - Brigid

To say I was shocked when my mask was fused to my face would be an understatement. But now I understood the heady incense that was being used. I kicked myself. I should have realized that the incense itself was a spell. There were plenty of other spells being held in here, but I thought it was wards to keep things secret or something. Stupid. I know. But clearly, I wasn't the only one surprised.

I heard his words, too. He's playing riddles with his words. He said we "will keep the secrets". Not that we "should" but that we "would". I don't like being controlled. But Brigittia and I knew that there were secrets here that we couldn't ferret out; forced secrets made sense then.

Speaking of Brigittia, I looked around to find her. Finally, as we were finding our tables, I saw her. She seemed heavily distracted by a blond-haired young man facing her. Looking at those shoulders and that back, I could see why. His mask sticks up just a little, with a tuft of some sort like a pointed ear and a fringe around his neck. He looks like a blond wolf. Wolf! Could he be my partner? Actually, he looks more like a lion. But maybe. Wait, am I wrong? Should I be a lion? Oh my goddess, this is so stressful!

He's going to sit down now and Brigittia doesn't seem to care. She's looking around for something. Apparently not even she has found her partner yet. That blond hunk seats himself so that he's facing Brigittia. My breath catches; my heart does this loopy, crazy beat. He is beautiful. Then there is a flash of pain on my wrist, like a thousand bee stings! I look down and I see a fine lined tattoo, like a bracelet, has appeared.

Fated mates tattoo. I. Have. A. Fated. Mates Tattoo.

I stumble backwards, catching myself against the chair behind me. I grab it behind me, holding on for dear life while the entire room tilts and spins. Someone is speaking to me, I realize through the buzzing in my ears. I shake my head, like a dog trying to dislodge a biting fly. Whoever it is repeats themself and this time I catch the end of what they're saying.

Twisting around, I realize the chair I grabbed was occupied, and the person sitting there is looking at me with concern.

"Sorry, just a moment of dizziness there. I'm so sorry to have bothered you."

"Well, that's understandable," the man with midnight black wings says. "Between this bewitching incense they doused us with, the spelled water, and then our masks fusing, it's been a bit much hasn't it?"

"Right. I'm a bit ashamed I didn't recognise more of the magic for what it was."

"Hmm," he was looking at me strangely, but then again, everyone was looking at people differently than they normally would. "May I help you back to your table? Do you know where you are sitting this evening?"

"No, thank you, I'll, I'll be fine."

"No, no, I insist. I wouldn't feel right if I let you fall." He paused a moment, as if debating something with himself. "Besides," he hesitated again, and I looked at him more carefully. "Besides, I think that young blond man over there, that captured your attention, I think we ought to walk by him. My instincts say that you are connected somehow."

I blink stupidly at him, probably looking again like an owl and not at all wolfish.

"What do you mean?"

"I'm not positive, but there is some sort of tether between you two, and I should like to see what it is. So let's walk to your table together. We can pretend to be old chums if you like, and I want to see if you and he feel this...thing, this bond too, as you are closer."

"Umm," I am not sure the last time I have ever felt this flustered since making a mistake on my oral history exam. "Um, yes, that seems reasonable. I would prefer to be ahead of the game on any more magic tonight."

He flashed me a smile, his teeth brilliant white against his dark skin. "Indeed."

Chapter 16 - Brigittia

After we were so unceremoniously dumped to the edges of the room, I tighten my energies to my wards. I keep being moved about with no control. I want every bit of protection I can muster. I had been saving those energies for later when I thought I might be tired. Now, I want to be sure I *get* to later. There is something underlying here that has my hackles up. I trust this evening less and less.

"Look," says a young red-haired woman in a mask of seashells near me, "we'll be dancing! That's what a ball is supposed to have and we'll be able to move about and meet more people!"

The music is delightful. Their volume is perfect, loud enough to easily recognize the waltz, but quiet enough to speak easily with those next to us.

I don't see any other masks that are owl-like except that man who walked in with me. I can't figure out what he is. I see him watching me, though. He seems calm through this chaos. I wonder if we might become friends.

That blond one, Thomas, now he is eye candy. He is still calm, too. He has a mask that is a bird of prey, I'm sure of it. Which is basically the same as an owl, especially since I don't see another like him. He must be my partner. Why else would I be so tongue tied around him?

"Hey," I say to seashell mask, "I'm Brigittia. Let's go find a dance partner."

"Yeah! Now that's what I'm talking about! I'm Seline." She grins and loops her arm through mine. I like the enthusiasm if not the volume.

She leans in and asks, "Have you seen who you think your partner is?"

"I'm not sure," I admit. "I have an idea of who it is, but we're not quite a perfect match."

She snorts, "How could we? These damn riddles were ridiculous. Is he wearing the right colors and metals?"

I mentally slap myself in the forehead. Of course, the animal part of the clue is only one third of it. "Hmm, I forgot those." I admit it to this strange girl. I don't think this admission weakens myself or my House. Not on an evening like this.

"So, does he?"

"Yeah, he has the silver, and the black is forefront. Yeah, we match!" I give a grin of my own. Her excitement is infectious.

"Great! We'll have you go to him in a moment. Help me find mine. I need blue and green and copper. My theme, as you can see, is under the sea."

"Hmmm," I look about. "I don't see any other seashells, but that man has a trident embroidered on his back. It's a reddish gold color, so maybe it's copper."

She followed my eyes and gripped my arm. "He does! Walk me over. Wait, where's your guy?"

I grinned, "It's fate. They are right beside each other."

We walked over, and as if they felt us, they both spun around. Sure enough, Mr Trident had on a teal shirt with a dark green sash with little seashells embroidered on it. He was handsome, too. Dark wavy hair and a bit of a scruff. He smiled at me, but flashed an even brighter smile at Selene. When we arrived beside them, Mr Trident said, "Want to dance, ladies?" Thomas held out his hand to me. I happily accepted it and slipped my hand into his. Immediately, I could feel the strength in his hand, and his little finger stroked over the callous on my palm. Apparently, we both were willing to work, but he didn't just have strength, he also had sensitivity.

We stepped out onto the floor and quickly joined the crowd, swirling and hopping through a number of dances. Thomas and I couldn't stop looking into each other's eyes and laughing together as we moved. It was too hard to dance well and say more than a few words, though.

"Let's sit a little, alright?" Thomas asked me.

"Indeed, we need a drink. But they took all the tables, remember?"

"Hmm, they seem to have put some out again. And drinks too."

We hurried over to a table draped with royal blue velvet. *Who puts velvet as a tablecloth?* And I was about to greedily drink a glass of wine when I suddenly hesitated.

"What is it? What's wrong?" asked Thomas, hesitating.

"I'm not sure." I paused, not sure what to say. "I think some of what happened before was magic, but also I think the drinks were drugged or spelled as well."

He blinked at me just like an owl. "Cobnobbits!" He set his mug down beside my glass. "You may be right. I'm so thirsty, too."

"Let me smell your beer. I can smell drugs better in beer than I can through heavy wine."

"You can smell drugs?" His eyebrows lifted farther up his forehead.

"Not very well. I'm trained to smell poisons, but they're similar, right?"

"Yeah, I guess."

So I picked up his glass and sniffed it, then swirled it and sniffed it more. I have a special symbol tattooed on the side of my thumb. I set it against his mug and let just a little of my energy into it. It didn't respond, suggesting there wasn't any magic in his mug. I set it back on the table and picked up my glass and tried the symbol touch again. Nothing.

"I don't know," I hissed. "I can't detect anything. Do we risk it?"

"I'm as thirsty as a horse. I'll try it," Thomas spoke without hesitation. We clinked our drinks and then drank deeply. Looking down on the velvet, I saw that the circles of wetness from our drinks just barely overlapped and made an infinity symbol. Surely it was a sign that we were meant to be partners and friends forever.

Chapter 17 - Thomas

This beautiful woman and her friend had come up to Thomas and the Mer beside him. Brigittia and Seline, apparently. Thomas could barely hold a coherent thought while Brigittia was near him, but then they danced and focussed only on each other. Quickly, Thomas found himself intrigued more by the woman's snappy wit than her obvious beauty.

They chucked at some of the garish masks and discussed their riddle.

"There was another gentleman here," Brigittia said while looking around for the black-winged fellow, "who mentioned how much he hated the ridiculousness of the riddles. I think I agree with him. At first I thought they were a decent test of intelligence, but the more people I have spoken with, the more similar sounding the riddles are and how easily one could find the wrong partner."

"Truly. I think the riddle is nearly as stressful as actually being here," agreed Thomas. "I didn't even want to attend, but my father expected it."

"Hmm, my parents didn't say much at all about it, but we guessed that I might receive an invitation."

Thomas pondered this. "You know," he said slowly, "there never seemed to be a question that I would receive an invitation. It was as if my dad knew all along."

"Really?"

"This whole ball is weird, y'know?"

"Yeah." She bit her lip and then decided to see just how much Thomas understood. "Do you know how the ball usually ends?"

"What do you mean?" Thomas was the most confused he had been all day. All day and all of this evening. "It ends with fireworks, right?"

"Hmm," Brigittia snorted. "But do you know what the last ceremony is?"

"Umm, no, I guess not particularly."

"Then you should know, too." Brigittia only thought it fair to warn him so he could bow out of a lifetime commitment if he wanted. "The last ceremony is-" but suddenly she couldn't speak. The words were literally held in her throat.

"The last ceremony is what?" asked Thomas, confusion painted across his features.

"I, I" Brigittia took a deep breath and tried again with no better success. "Apparently, I can't tell you what the last ceremony is."

"You can't tell me, like it's a secret you can't share?"

"Well um, yes. I guess. But it's not that I don't want to tell you, the words literally, I mean I, I, *can't* say the words!"

"Huh?"

"It's magic. I literally can't say it."

"You know," says Thomas heatedly, "I don't mind magic, but tonight has been a bit much. This whole ball is a bit much!"

"I agree," murmured Brigittia. "I go back to my previous assessment, when I only knew what I had been taught about this tradition. I didn't want a part of it then or now." Thinking of another angle, she then said, "How much did you learn about this from your teachers?"

At the same time, Thomas said flirtatiously, "But if you hadn't come, we wouldn't have met."

Brigittia couldn't help it, she smiled back at him, face warm and her heart beating faster. "You're right."

"Learn from my teachers? I'm not sure I ever did. I mean, I guess I learned it's a tradition and that it helps Houses and Kingdoms make alliances."

Her jump of happiness fading slightly, Brigittia prompted, "Uhhuh, but how do they strengthen or make those alliances?"

"I dunno. Through bargains and agreements, and friendships."

"Or more than friendships?"

"I, I guess."

Thomas was confused by this conversation, but it seemed that this beautiful woman wanted him to figure something out. If she had been his mother, he would have been irritated, but just as he started to feel frustrated, he remembered that there was magic working against her. She wanted him to understand. It had to be an important idea if the magic was trying to hold it back. Still, she smiled so prettily when he flirted. That's all he wanted to do.

A burning sensation encircled his wrist then, like a hundred bees stinging him all at once. Brigittia gasped too and began rubbing her wrist.

"What the Hades?!" Thomas exclaimed.

"What the-" Brigittia's words froze on her lips as she heard Thomas and looked at his face. Her eyes shot down to his wrist then.

Thomas followed her line of sight to his wrist and then to her, holding her own wrist. He gently reached forward and peeled her fingers away from her wrist. He locked eyes with her and held his wrist beside hers. Both had fine lined tattoos inked on their wrists. Thomas' looked like an interwoven chain, Brigittia's like a dainty vine wrapping around her wrist, leaves trailing down to the back of her hand.

"You know what this is?" breathed Thomas.

"Yeah," Brigittia bit her lip and then quickly released it, holding his gaze. "You know what it means?"

"Yeah."

"So the last ceremony tonight is about this."

"You mean-"

"Yeah, we get-" again the words were caught in her throat. "Our Houses will be forever linked."

Thomas grinned, and Brigittia smiled widely, too.

Then there was a commotion through the crowd as other guests began clutching their wrists and crying out in pain.

Thomas and Brigittia glanced around and then smiled back at each other.

"I guess we were just ahead of the curve," said Thomas.

"Yeah." Brigittia slipped her hand into his and turned to stand beside him, watching the crowd.

The buzz of the crowd was getting louder and emotions ran higher as not everyone was thrilled to be branded with a mate bond.

Thomas leaned over and said into her ear, "Let's go for a walk outside."

"Can we still?" asked Brigittia.

Thomas snorted a laugh. "True, let's see if we can."

That rule hadn't changed at least, and the two and several others slipped out the doors into the quiet night.

"I'm sure there are magic barriers to keep us here, but let's see if we can walk the gardens," suggested Brigittia.

The fireworks continued their loud booms and splattering lights. Slowly, the cloud of smoke from the burnt fireworks created a haziness. Silently slipping in on silver paws, fog slowly crept over the grass and moved everyone closer together. Before he realized it, Thomas was elbow to elbow and shoulder to shoulder in the crowd. The back of his throat began to burn, but whether from the raw smoke of the fireworks or the spicy incense, he wasn't sure. Thomas was momentarily distracted by the gorgeous blooms of light while he contemplated why they would want to burn incense outside. He tugged an ear in thought. A particularly loud boom vibrated his very sternum and drew his attention back to the sky.

Suddenly, the sky erupted with more brilliant lights and colors with thunderous booms, and more magical delight than Thomas could have ever imagined. Those around him gasped with appreciation, too.

Thomas could not have described the awe-inspiring glorious burst of colors if he had tried.

Then, as the last colors dripped from the sky and darkness returned, it was as if a black velvet curtain was dropped upon the crowd. Sounds were muffled, and while not restrained, no one could move. Whispers started and muttering increased, but Thomas wondered if it wasn't really people screaming and shouting, just muted by the heavy darkness. In the blink of an eye, sound returned, and he was literally standing in front of a tall, crimson, velvet curtain. Quickly looking left and right, Thomas saw that he and apparently every other male guest was lined up and evenly spaced, facing this curtain. He tried to take a step back and see more, but his eyebrows shot up in surprise as he found his feet were rooted to the ground.

"Light preserve us!" growled a dark-skinned man to his left. His wings stretched out as he obviously tried to move backwards, too. "They've trapped us here. Why? What now?"

"This entire ball is a setup," agreed Thomas, "but I don't know what we're being set up for!"

The man glanced right towards him. "You don't?"

Thomas wrinkled his forehead. "No. You do?"

"Hmm." The man had stopped struggling to move backwards and his wings settled again. Gorgeous black feathers with a bluish sheen on them caught glints of starlight. He flashed a grin at Thomas. "You have noticed the fated mate's ink on your wrist, right?"

"Uhhuh." Thomas ground his teeth in frustration. "It's why I'm not worried about the riddles any more. I found a gorgeous woman here and then the mark appeared. She is the center of all my heart seeks. Whether we're riddle partners or not, we'll be together."

"Indeed. And unless I miss my guess, the officiant is about to make that announcement right now."

"What?"

The man grunted, then coughed uncomfortably. "There is a particular ceremony that I want to tell you about but seems to be magically caught in my throat so I can't tell you what to expect, what is about to happen. You are indeed about to be with your fated mate."

"Really?" Thomas' face broke into a huge, silly grin. All his concern melted away, and he turned back to the curtain, excited to be with Brigittia again.

The man narrowed his eyes at Thomas. Something didn't feel right, more than just the magical incense affecting everything.

A ripple moved through the curtain, and the host began to speak again with his magically amplified voice. "Midnight breaks upon us, my honored guests, and brings us to the most important traditions of the night. A few of you have known what the next ceremony is, but could not share the information with your new friends. I apologize for that, but it is a tradition to keep it mostly a secret until the last moment. The good news is that soon you will be baring all!" He laughed a little too loudly. "Sorry, sorry. In truth, this makes me a little uncomfortable, too. But please understand that these choices made for the next ceremony were made with a great deal of thought or money to create the best result for your Houses, and your Families, and your very kingdoms."

Whisperings swirled around the curtain from both sides, and Thomas realized the females were also on the other side, evenly spaced out like the men.

"Without further ado, let me introduce the man of the hour," Thomas imagined their host stepping back and waving some important person forward, "our Ceremony Officiant." Hesitant clapping started, and then everyone joined in.

"Hmhm," a new and gravelly voice cleared his throat and began. "Welcome, honored guests! It pleases me to be the one to be here tonight. Tonight marks an auspicious day in your lives, forever sealing you and your partner together for the rest of your lives. Many of you believe that you have found your riddle partner. I'm happy for you. In a moment, this crimson curtain will lift and reveal your partner. A few of you may be surprised, but as you all know, you are fated to be together. Your wrists show that."

At these words, Thomas let loose a sigh of relief. He and Brigittia were partners, after all. They would have plenty of time to get to know each other and stop stumbling over their words.

"I will remind you, and some of you need to listen carefully, a fated mate does not a heart mate make."

There was silence for a moment following this warning. Then fresh whispers.

"When the curtain lifts, you will step forward and take your mate's hands in yours, and then face me to take your vows."

Vows!? Thomas' heart dropped, then soared. He had no idea what vows, but he and Brigittia would be hand fasted in some sort of way if they were to hold hands and take a vow together.

The crimson curtain slowly began to rise. Blindfolds appeared, tied snugly over their masks. Thomas couldn't see a thing except a sliver of light over one cheekbone.

Chapter 18 - Aetherius

I lost sight of my mate just after the dancing started. Some idiot spilled their drink down my arm. I found a washroom without too much difficulty and washed up. I hate to be sticky. Then I used some strange contraption on their wall to blow hot air against my sleeve and mostly dry it. I don't know what this machine was, but it had a fan blowing hot air and I imagine it would dry hands quite quickly. It did tolerably well on my sleeve. At least I was more comfortable.

I returned to the crowd on the dance floor, but I couldn't see her anymore. Nonetheless, I do enjoy dancing and I was getting eyes from quite a few of the ladies. I chose some who I was obviously not partnered with, and we enjoyed a number of dances. Their conversational ability varied vastly, but overall, I heartily agreed with all of them that these damn riddles were proving quite incomprehensible to many of the guests.

I suspected that it wouldn't matter. We had been whisked around all night by magic. I couldn't imagine that errors between partner matches would be allowed. I decided I might as well enjoy myself and relax. I knew who my lady was and worse case scenario, I would find her by pulling every couple apart until I found her. The last ceremony tonight would be a success for me. Meanwhile, I could enjoy the dancing. I truly didn't find it unpleasant sliding my hands across the backs of beautiful women and not a few of them pressed up close and let me grope their ass as well. A few offered to test the mobility of their masks in a back room with me, but those offers I politely refused. I didn't want to tarnish myself and come to my mate dirty. That seemed unnecessarily rude. I would be upset if she did that to me, and I fully believed we should respect each other equally. We were not destined to fall in love, but we were destined for a partnership. It wouldn't be easily successful if we started out with an argument. It would be best if we could trust and respect each other. Friendship would be ideal, too.

About a half hour before midnight, I began to notice a musky scent in the air. While I couldn't smell spells, I guessed there was magic in the incense again. I paused from the dancing for a glass of cold cider with hat peppers floating in it. Spicy and cold, it was delicious. It heated my belly as it cooled my throat. I quickly gulped it down and asked for another. I took this glass to the wide doors thrown open at the end of the hall. Strangely, the incense was just as strong here where there should have been fresh air, but I did enjoy a cool breeze upon my cheeks. I stepped out and leaned against a column. I guessed it held a balcony to a higher story. It gave me a pleasant view of the darkened grounds and the starry sky.

"You're in a perfect spot, m'lord," a young man spoke to me. He wore House Everhart colors, but I couldn't tell his role.

"Oh, yeah?" I asked.

"Indeed. The fireworks will begin soon. It's almost midnight."

"Ah, yes." I spoke politely, but internally I snorted with laughter. Oh yes, I imagined there would be a lot of fireworks at midnight. That's when we should all be paired up with our preordained partners, and then there would be the last ceremony resulting in more...fireworks.

"Fireworks before the last ceremony?" I asked him.

"Yes, m'lord. The fireworks lead to the official pairing of the riddle partners."

"I see." I hid a smile in my glass. The official pairing. It sounded so proper when he said it. I wondered how much he knew.

"You know," he whispered, "I have never been to one of these balls, but I hear the last ceremony is stupendous. I can't wait to watch!"

"I'm sure it does sound exciting. I'm not sure if you can though, or if it will be one of those carefully kept secrets. No one ever talks about it."

"Oh." He immediately deflated. "You're right, I didn't think of that. I probably won't be able to watch." He smiled at me then, "I hope you enjoy it, m'lord. Think of me while you do."

"Oh, I hope to enjoy it. Thank you." *But I won't be thinking of you.*

The musky scent grew heavier and intermixed with some flower scents, roses maybe, and something sweeter. There was almost a wine-like taste in the air, too. Even I was beginning to feel a little lightheaded, I couldn't imagine what the weaker species were feeling. My demon blood gave me a little buffer of protection. There was nothing left in my glass, so I set it down on the railing and rubbed my face. Even the tips of my ears were tingling. Was it the hot pepper in the cider doing this, or was it the magic that I was sure was swirling around?

Chapter 19 - Brigid

It seemed like there were a hundred people out in the gardens and on the verandas. Brigid drank some cold juice and breathed deeply the needed cool, fresh air after dancing so much. Her feet hurt from dancing and being passed from one partner to another. Her cheeks hurt too from all the laughter and smiling. She did love to dance!

Brigid's parents paid for dancing lessons for her and her sister when they were younger. It helped at the many formal dances her mother, the senator, was invited to over the years. She could hold her own through any dance with any dignitary's son. Even if she didn't know the steps to a dance, and sometimes there were foreign dances, she could always fake it well enough to look effortless so that she and her partner managed fine. Much better than many of the clumsy boys she had been paired with over the years. Eventually, though, those fun lessons ended and now there seemed to be political negotiations before anyone was allowed to ask her to dance at any of her mother's parties. Brigid missed those parts of just being a kid.

How ironic, then, that this night of politics would let her let go completely again and dance with whomever she pleased. This ball was fun once she let go of finding her partner. These riddles were hard. Once more of the guests had partnered up, it should be easier for her to find her partner. She hadn't found him while dancing, but she was sure she would soon.

Quickly enough, her breathing slowed down. Brigid tipped her head back and looked up at the skies. Stars were everywhere; despite the lights spread around the gardens, she could see them clearly. A slight brush of wind blew a strand of hair across her mask. It was weird how she could feel it, like the mask had fused to her face so completely that it acted like her own skin.

Brigid spun suddenly when the magic amplified the host's voice.

"Thank you, once again my friends, for being here tonight!" He paused while the talking quieted down. "I hope you have enjoyed our delicious foods, finest wines and spirits, and cooled off from the fantastic dancing with fresh juices and water."

Brigid finished the last of her juice and with a smile, set it on a waiter's empty tray as he passed.

"If we could now have everyone come outside for a special display?"

"Fireworks!" was whispered up and down the verandas and Brigid could hear it being whispered inside as well.

First a trickle of guests and then a flood of people came out the doors and pushed Brigid and the others out on the lawns. Friends began calling out to each other and standing in familiar groups. Brigid looked around but didn't see anyone she recognised. She couldn't find any of the guests from her table, or her childhood friend, Brigittia, not even the handsome blond. She wished Skye was there. Skye would sit at attention beside her, and Brigid would brush her fingers through her coarse hair on her head and stroke her soft ears. Just Skye's presence could soothe her and give her strength. But Skye wasn't here, and Brigid nervously clenched and unclenched her fingers instead.

There was a crackling, a hissing, and a whine. Immediately followed by bright lights bursting in the sky overhead and a thunderous boom. The excited whispers had been right and fireworks lit up Kalifornia's night sky.

The chattering stopped almost entirely as everyone tipped their faces up to the sky. Burst after burst of colored lights lit up the sky. Suddenly, Brigid realized how vulnerable she and everyone were just staring up at the sky. She immediately dropped her gaze and scanned around her. She saw a few others doing the same, but most guests were just awestruck and mesmerized by the spattering, colorful lights and terrible booms.

Strange shadows moved within the windows of the hall and a breeze suddenly carried a heady incense smell out. Brigid's brow furrowed as she tried to understand what was happening. Why would they need that heady incense again? Surely the fireworks were the celebration of a long night? But no, the host had mentioned staying until dawn? Brigid was so confused.

The fireworks continued on and Brigid looked up again. She was awestruck by these. She had seen fireworks at many fancy houses and political gatherings, but none had been this fancy. No longer were they bursting one at a time, but now two or three at a time and new ones erupting as the prior faded and spread. The entire sky was filled with brilliant colors and speeding lights. Her nose itched with the burning smoke hazing the air. Her ears held a faint ringing from the repeated booms shuddering her entire body.

A pounding started to echo in her temples from the overwhelming flashes, acrid smoke, incense, and thunderous noise. Brigid wished she could remove her mask. She rolled her neck and shoulders, then pinched the bridge of her nose.

"Harsh isn't it?" Brigittia spoke quietly into her ear. Brigid jumped in surprise, but no fear when her friend surprised her.

"Oh my, this is a bit overwhelming. It's so loud, and flashing-do you smell that incense again?"

"No, I-" Brigittia stopped short as the breeze shifted and brought a whiff of the heavy incense to them. "Oh, I see. Last time, I thought that carried a spell. What is being done now?"

"I don't know, but I don't trust this."

"No, you shouldn't," agreed Brigittia. "We have to keep our guard up."

The fireworks continued, and slowly the cloud of smoke from the burnt fireworks created a haziness. Silently slipping in on silver paws, a fog slowly crept over the grass and moved the partygoers closer together.

Brigid and Brigittia stood back to back, both subconsciously dropping a hand as if to touch their pet wolves.

Brigid didn't understand. One moment, she was outside watching the most brilliant fireworks she had ever seen. Then, she felt like she was suffocating under a heavy softness of complete darkness. Before she could panic, although her hand was on her dagger, she was in a line of females staring at a heavy, crimson curtain. Taking a step back almost had her fall on her butt as her feet could not move. She threw her arms out for balance and slightly windmilled her weight forward again. To her relief, she saw others doing the same or similar up and down the line to her left and right. One poor girl did actually fall and awkwardly stood back up again. The woman next to her, who had strong feline characteristics, tried to reach a hand down to help her, but was too far away to reach a hand. They were each spaced quite evenly and just out of reach.

Brigid could hear the fast breathing of a young woman to her left, who sounded very close to panic. Upon closer inspection, Brigid was relieved to see Brigittia to her right. Brigittia gave her a tight smile and then cocked her head to better listen to their host.

"Midnight breaks upon us, my honored guests, and brings us to the most important traditions of the night. A few of you have known what the next ceremony is..." Brigid heard Brigittia give a rather unladylike snort.

"Do you know more than me?" Brigid asked her friend.

"Only a little. And I haven't been able to tell you, though I did try damned hard." Brigittia looked angry, which had Brigid's stomach churning in apprehension.

"Why?"

"This may be a bit more..." Brigittia seemed to struggle to speak, "permanent than you expected."

"Huh?"

"You'll see."

"...our Ceremony Officiant." Their host sounded like he was introducing someone new, but since Brigid couldn't see far enough down the line to see him, it meant nothing.

An unknown voice began speaking. His voice was calm and strong, gravelly and sure. It calmed her a little from Brigittia's strange attitude.

Brigid only half listened as she tried to puzzle this out. She clearly heard him say, "I will remind you, and some of you need to listen carefully: a fated mate does not a heart mate make." That sounded like a warning and had Brigid clutching her dagger until her knuckles were white.

"Psst," Brigittia was motioning to her. "Put that away, tuck it wherever you hid it before. You do NOT want to be seen with a weapon right now. Keep it handy, though."

Brigid wasn't sure her head or her stomach could handle much more of this tense stress. It was excruciating, and it was not enjoyable anymore.

The powerful male voice continued, "When the curtain lifts, you will step forward and take your mate's hands in yours, and then face me to take your vows."

Vows!? Vows of what? To be best friends forevermore, to be trading partners, what? Brigid rubbed her temples and surreptitiously sniffed the lavender on her wrist to calm herself.

Brigid became aware of movement behind them. Glancing back, she saw cute little canvas cabanas.

"Look, we'll have some privacy to talk," she smiled at Brigittia then. Surely they were stressed for no reason. No one had ever said there was anything bad, let alone terrible, that happened at the ball.

Brigittia narrowed her eyes at the tented, 3-sided enclosures. "No way," she breathed. "They don't close?"

"Now that would be inappropriate, wouldn't it?" giggled Brigid. She could have sworn she saw her friend roll her eyes.

"I'm sorry, Brigid. But you're strong, you'll be fine."

"What?"

The crimson curtain slowly began to rise. Invisible hands seemed to quickly dab her neck, arms, and chest with a warm, dampened cloth. Then, those invisible hands worked deftly to smooth her hair, pulling it back loosely and maybe plaiting it. She was urged to take a mint in her mouth. Lastly, blindfolds appeared, tied snugly over their masks. Now Brigid was glued to the floor, out of reach of anyone, and blind. She felt very vulnerable. Whispers ran up and down the line. Panic soured the air. A draft swirled around Brigid's ankles and the heady smell of the incense increased. She felt more than she knew that the curtain was waist high and then at shoulder height and then somewhere above her head. She craned her neck this way and that, trying to see anything out from under her blindfold, but all she accomplished was to begin to feel a little dizzy.

What did Brigittia know that she didn't? Her riddle partner was the strong blond, right? They hadn't even talked business, or lands, or anything. How could they make vows on anything yet?!

But then, a calm enveloped her as she remembered they could not leave until dawn. They still had hours before that. No wonder the cabanas had appeared. They would need time alone to talk. Absently, she rubbed the new tattoo, the fated mate's bond, on her wrist. It brought a smile to her lips, and she loosed a deep breath.

Chapter 20 - The Ceremony - Aetherius

"Reach forward and find your partner's hands."

I knew better than to blindly follow the officiant's words and yet my hands moved of their own accord. I groped forward blindly and found her strong fingers reaching forward. We grasped onto each other like blind men in a thunderstorm, and once we had a grip, we didn't let go.

I struggled to say something, anything, to her, but the words were held in my throat. My wings raised and lowered in agitation. I was really tired of all this magic. I smiled as I heard her growl. She must be having the same struggle. I squeezed her hands with two quick squeezes, but never let go. I heard her chuckle as she gave me a squeeze back. She was such a perfect mate for me.

The officiant droned on about strength through our partners and from shared experiences like this. The scent of fear was rising, despite how the incense was proportionally increased. Before long, any of the more sensitive noses like werewolves would keel over.

In my heart, I knew we could be powerful partners, but only if she chooses to be my partner like that. Otherwise, this might be slightly more than convenience, respect, and maybe friendship. I want the former with this beautiful woman, I realized. But I came into this expecting the latter. Either will be made to work. As long as she bears my heirs, I don't care what she does during the rest of her time. But together, we could be amazing!

I can hear her breathing quickening. I wonder if she knows the scope of events tonight. I feel like she does. She smells nervous but not scared. I can't read her thoughts. I did delve in to see what she was thinking. I rarely do that without just cause or permission, but this whole words-locked-in-the-throat changes the rules, right? She has powerful wards. It was like hitting a marble wall. Given enough time with water and a diamond drill, I might work my way in, but by then she would have enough notice to just build another wall. She gave a shiver as I pulled back, like she had felt me. It must just be coincidence. No one has ever felt me when I slip in.

"-will be married for evermore. These are not relationships lightly taken, nor will you ever dissolve these vows. You are linked from now until forever-" The rest of the officiant's words were lost in a hurricane of gasps and shrieks from those startled by the news. My lady did neither, nor did her posture or scent change. She knew. I don't know how a fae mortal knew, but she had known.

Magic raised the officiant's voice as he continued to speak. "You may lean forward and kiss your spouse, then you will retire to your cabanas to solidify the relationship."

My lady gasped at that. "No privacy!" I heard her murmur. She was right. There were but three sides to any of these cabanas, and I would guess official observers, too.

I felt a squeeze in her fingers as she leaned forward, I gently squeezed back and leaned forward. Our faces bumped a little as we had no depth perception being blindfolded, but quickly my mouth found her hot lips. We both sucked in a little breath as we smelled and tasted each other for the first time. She smelled of wild roses, not the overly sweet garden variety but wild ones, and tasted of berries and fruit with a dash of something spicy. I raised my hand to her face, holding her naked cheek. I felt movement around us as other couples shrieked and tried to move away. Our feet were still firmly held in place. The couple to my left thrashed a great deal, and I loosely encircled up with my wings to keep away their flailing limbs.

I felt her smile and then stiffen. Just then, our blindfolds disappeared and our masks dropped. I saw her eyes widen as she took in my face.

"You?!" she gasped.

I tilted my head. "Indeed."

"But, I,-" she paused and glanced around. Her grip on my hand never faltered, indeed her other hand grasped our held hands, too. I brought my hand from her cheek down to our twined fingers. "Oh." was all she said when she saw blondy beside us with her friend. "They aren't the same." She was looking at his mate bond inked on his wrist. Her thumb rubbed my wrist as she looked down. Our mate bonds were identical.

"Did you know?" she asked softly. "When we walked in together, did you know then?" A tear slipped down her cheek.

I raised my hand up to her cheek again and gently thumbed it away, before slipping my hand under her chin and lifting her head to make eye contact. "I didn't know then, but soon after."

"Oh."

"You knew about the marriage?" I asked.

"Yeah." Her tone was even and controlled. "I knew my partner was forever, but I thought, I mean, He, I-"

"Hush," I whispered. Just then, our feet were released from the floor's hold. "Come, sit. Let's breathe and re-adjust." I led us to our cabana.

She hesitated a little, seeing the only furniture was a bed and a small table with a pitcher of water. Nonetheless, her maturity was no less than her courage and she walked in and slid up to sit on the bed, leaving me space to sit beside her. I poured out a glass of water first and offered it to her.

She took it gratefully. "Thank you. My throat is raw from the incense and probably the fireworks, too."

"Mine too," I said. "And I'm Aetherius, by the way."

"Oh!" she started, "I'm sorry, I'm Brigittia. Pleasure to...meet you."

"Indeed. It is a pleasure to know you better." I poured a second glass and drank heavily from it before sitting next to her. Looking out, I saw our official observer. At least they had some decency. She was standing across the way instead of right by our cabana. She offered the illusion of privacy, despite holding a notebook and a watch. We made eye contact. She gave me a small smile and nod. I saluted her with my glass.

"Who is that?" asked Brigittia, still observant, if in a slight state of shock.

"I would hazard a guess that she is the one to mark when we have finished the ceremony."

"Oh." Her cheeks flushed a deep red. I knew she knew what was expected. Unlike many of the sobs and shrieking, not just female, around us. It seemed she had come to this night mentally prepared.

She took a deep breath, another sip of water, and suddenly had a warrior's calm about her.

"It took some digging for me to find out how this ceremony ends, but the marriage I was taught about at a young age. I am mostly prepared. My brain is, at least. And you seem kind. Thank you." She spoke softly but calmly, with strength in her voice.

"I think it is entirely fair to be nervous. There is not a time requirement that I know of, except that we must be ready to leave at dawn."

"Yes. Ok." She held out one hand then, open on the bed. I shifted my drink to the other hand and then gently set my hand on hers.

For a fleeting moment, it was as if her guards were down and I could feel and hear her thoughts, but on a delay.

This was not what I expected. I knew there were plenty of unknowns for the ball. I knew we would have a marriage, but nothing could have prepared me for this. My journal entries would be far more detailed. I smiled briefly at the thought. That's when this dark, winged stranger raised his glass to a woman across the room. She smiled and nodded at us.

"Who is that?"

"I would hazard a guess that she is the one to mark when we have finished the ceremony."

"Oh." My cheeks heated. But he didn't comment on my blush and I pulled myself together. We sipped our water.

"Did you know what to expect?" he asked me.

I swallowed a chuckle. "It took some digging for me to find out how this ceremony ends, but the marriage I was taught about at a young age. I am mostly prepared. My brain is, at least. And you seem kind. Even though you aren't- thank you."

"I think it is entirely fair to be nervous. There is not a time requirement that I know of, except that we must be ready to leave at dawn."

He was right. I bit my cheek, wishing for whiskey instead of water. He was kind enough to let me set the pace, but there was no escaping this. Nor, however much I wished, would we be able to change this. I had been so certain that Thomas was my partner. We both had the ink on our wrists, our fated mate's bonds. He was handsome, he was funny; we had shared a conversation about books...It was time to move forward on this path instead. I laid down my hand on the bed between us. He smiled and set his hand on mine and laced our fingers together again.

Heat pushed out from his hand and against mine, but my wards were holding it just off my body. It surrounded me like the heat trapped beneath a blanket. His eyebrows lifted in surprise.

"Your magic-" he started, just as I said "What family do you-"

We both chuckled, and some tension evaporated.

"Ladies first," he said.

"Thanks." I licked my lips to try to find the right words. "I don't know how to ask this without sounding rude, but I don't mean to be-"

"I think most people tonight are a little flustered. It's fine. Ask me."

I nodded and took another sip of water. "What family are you from? I have never been close to someone with wings before, and I don't recognize your features at all. Usually I can place the eyes of famous families."

"Eyes are windows to the soul, they say," he murmured. "And yours are beautiful."

I felt my cheeks warm again, but he continued on.

"I am not surprised that you don't recognize my features. Nor my species, I think you were dancing around. I have the advantage. I came here knowing my partner was fae." He sipped his water again. "The short answer is that you do not know me, because we are not welcome in your lands, usually. I am a demon, technically, but really a Eudaemon. Have you heard of us?"

"Eudaemons are known as good demons, right? Or light demons?"

She was well educated. I smiled in relief. This would be much easier. "Yes, we are the Light demons, or the good demons. Truly, there are good and evil in any species-"

"Yes," she agreed.

"But we are the protectors. We may use power and strength to overcome the evil of the world, but we do it for the greater good."

"Are your species not responsible for creating truces and war treaties?"

"Yes."

And we are partnered. Why? I don't have any sort of power or clout on par with that?"

I smiled wide. "I love how intelligent you are. Most people, men and women, would still be trying to find a way out of a forced marriage to a stranger or to a demon. You are trying to figure out why we are partnered."

She snorted a laugh. "It's what I do. I analyze everything." She grinned wickedly. "Want to know what else I already thought of?"

I raised an eyebrow and grinned back, "Yes, yes, I do."

"We may not have privacy for when we consummate this marriage, but I have more than most since you have these gorgeous wings." She reached out gently to stroke the top of my wing. Energy danced from her fingers down and across my feathers, creating a web of tingles that didn't fade until she pulled her finger back.

I laughed. "I shall do my best to protect your modesty, though that clipboard woman has to see enough to be satisfied." She nodded, and I continued. "My turn to ask a question."

Brigittia unbuckled, then kicked off her shoes, wiggling her toes in pleasure at the freedom. She surprised me then, as she moved to sit on my lap facing me as she placed her glass on the little table.

"I assume you won't judge me too forward as I try to move past my shyness." She shook her hair loose, and finger combed it back. The tips of her ears were slightly pointed, as were her canines, as she smiled at me. "Ask."

I blinked at her for a moment, and to my utter discomfort felt myself get hard beneath her. She grinned as she felt that.

"I'm sorry," I said as I tried to shift her off my lap.

"No, it's fine. Actually, it's a compliment, right? Ask me your question."

She was a fae, but damn if she wasn't also a wolf ready to hunt and lead her pack. Or maybe protect her pack, I wasn't sure.

I cleared my throat and took a sip of water before setting my glass beside hers. I raised my hands to gently hold her waist. "What is your magic?"

She blinked in confusion. "My magic? What do you mean? My runes?"

"No, I don't think it's just runes. You hold magic within you."

She chuckled then, "No, I think my life would be different if I had magic. I might have choices then." She bit her lip, momentarily saddened. Then she met my eyes again. Courageous this one. Intelligent, full of laughter, and courageous. "I have enough energy to hold the runes longer or to charge one more than the others for a short time, but I don't have magic."

"I think you do." I whispered. "I have never felt someone with *energy* like you."

"What do you mean?"

"Usually, my gifts allow me to read a person when we touch. I can know their general thoughts and feelings, but with you there is a buffer that bounces my energy back at me. But when you initiate the touch, when you touched my wing a moment ago, it's like flames tickling across me. No one has done that to me for centuries. The last time I felt it was a powerful priestess."

Her eyes had widened in surprise. "Centuries?! How old are you?" She clapped a hand over her mouth. "Light, that was dreadfully rude. I mean-"

"Shh. It's fine. Honest discourse is never rude. Uncouth maybe, but never rude. Intention matters, I guess I mean."

"I'm sorry, you caught me by surprise," she took a deep breath. "I'm about to reach my 23rd year. How old are you?"

By the light, she was a babe, even by fae standards. But I had to remember she also had human blood in her. "Eudaemons have a very long life span, but by our standards, I am young, like you. Well, a little more, maybe more, like almost thirty years." I felt her tension relaxing. "That being the case, I am about 430 years old."

"Four hundred-" her voice trailed off, then she continued. "You must have traveled a great deal. I'm jealous. I look forward to you telling me more accurate stories of history. The books tend to be...unreliable."

I leaned forward and kissed her gently on the lips. I pulled back and leaned my forehead against hers. "I'll be happy to share all the history I know. But I want to know more about this energy you have."

"I wonder," she murmured, "our family does come from the Isle of Avalon, but I was taught those were just stories."

"More than stories, the best stories are always based on truths."

"Indeed." Her eyes lit up then. "Do you know where to find the dragons?"

I chuckled deep and nipped her bottom lip. "We're going to have fun, you and I."

"Yes," she replied, a sudden tear slipping down her cheek.

Chapter 21 - Brigid

What the Light is happening? Like really?!

W
hat the Light is happening? Like really?!
I'm so overwhelmed, so confused. I can't breathe, my chest is tight, my face is hot. Thomas is finally looking at me and he isn't looking at me. He's not happy to be partnered with me. He's all I wanted for a partner tonight, and he doesn't want me. I suspect that our partnership isn't just tonight. I'm so dumb! So stupidly naïve. This is what Brigittia was trying to tell me, that tonight ends in marriage. And I'm the lucky one. I get the man of my dreams. She has some weird-looking guy with wings. But Thomas doesn't want me. It's painfully obvious.

I need to be strong, but I just want to collapse and cry. This is everything I hoped for and everything that could go wrong.

Brigid could feel herself spiraling into panic. She bit her cheek hard to ground herself and tasted the coppery blood. Her cheek would be swollen and irritated in the morning. Just like her heart.

Brigid took a deep breath and then focused on breathing slowly in through her nose and out through her mouth. A warrior's technique. If this wasn't a battle of sorts, she didn't know what was. Politics and her heart weren't working together, but this time she had to focus on everything to win at both. A quick glance over showed that Brigittia had white spots on her cheekbones, but she was outwardly calm. She was only looking at her partner, not at Thomas. Thomas was the one who wasn't calm. His breathing was coming in ragged breaths like a fearful colt. His head was thrashing about with wide eyes, as if he looked around enough he could find salvation. There wasn't salvation. Brigid knew with a sinking pit in her chest that there was no salvation except what she made right now. He might only have eyes for Brigittia right now, but she would make him hers. They were fated mates. She had the universe on her side.

Brigid squeezed Thomas' hands. "Look at me," she hissed.

"No, but," his ragged breathing didn't soften his voice, "there is a mistake. This whole thing is a mistake!"

"No, it's not. Look at me." Brigid continued to speak softly and rubbed her thumb on the back of his hand. "Look at me. We'll get through this, but we're a team now. We have to work together."

"Brigittia!" Thomas cried out and tried to lunge sideways, but their feet were still rooted to the floor.

Brigittia blinked quickly, but didn't even look at him.

"Stop it!" hissed Brigid. "Do not make a scene. We are partners, dammit. Look at me."

Thomas looked at Brigid with wide eyes, and she knew he wasn't really seeing her.

Brigid hissed, "Thomas, listen to me. WE are partners, not you and Brigittia. You and I are fated mates, not you and her. She won't even look at you. Look at me!"

Slowly, Thomas stopped throwing his head about. His wide eyes met hers and slowly cleared.

"Yes, but, but. I love her. She's perfect, she's my partner-wait, she's not my partner?"

"No."

"No."

"We're partners, you and I?"

Brigid lifted an eyebrow. "Yes." At least the review session was going fairly quickly.

"And this partnership is forever?"

"Yes."

"But I love her."

"You just met her. You don't love her."

"I do."

"Whatever, but we can grow to love each other."

"I can't."

"We'll be married. We can figure it out."

"Married, but-"

"But nothing. We don't have a choice."

"But," he sighed in despondent acceptance. "Right, I guess this is foreordained. We can be friends, Brigid, and be partners."

"Yes, and love can grow from friendship."

Thomas had come back to his senses now. "Right, we can be partners. True love has little to do with most marriages, right?"

Brigid smiled gently. "Right."

"But umm, we still have an issue," said Thomas hesitantly.

Brigid furrowed her brow, but then windmilled her arms as their feet were suddenly loosed. Thomas gently caught her as she almost fell.

"Whoa, easy there." Thomas looked around again and saw everyone able to move again. "Look, I think this cabana is set up for us to have some privacy."

They stepped towards it and then faltered as they saw it only contained a bed.

"No way!" breathed Thomas.

"I think we have to...consummate this marriage," faltered Brigid.

Thomas held back, eyes wide again, but Brigid took a breath and stepped forward, tugging Thomas by the hand she still held.

"Is there no choice?" he whispered.

"I don't think so," answered Brigid in a low voice. "The ceremony man, the officiant, made it sound very permanent and very immediate."

"Yeah."

"You're beautiful, Brigid," Thomas said, facing her, "and it has nothing to do with that. But I think I may close my eyes and imagine us far, far, far away from here in another place and another time."

"Another person too?"

"I, well, honestly?"

"Honestly."

"Then yes. I always expected to choose my bride, not have her thrust at me. No offense."

"No. No offense taken." A tear slipped down Brigid's cheek, but she appreciated his honesty.

"Brigid, this isn't fair to either of us, but especially to you!" Thomas' voice was anguished as they stepped into the cabana and next to the bed. "You're being so brave and kind, and calm. I'm not worthy of you. You deserve someone better and someone who will truly love you, because I cannot. I love someone else."

"We both deserve more," Brigid answered, her voice breaking. She sat heavily on the bed, face in her hands, and let the tears fall.

Thomas stared for a moment, unsure what to do with his bride. Finally, he knelt in front of her and pulled her against his shoulder. He didn't hate her, but he didn't love her. It was not she that he wanted in this cabana. She leaned against him and cried silently, slowly soaking his shirt with her tears.

Brigid had been so uncomfortable at the ceremony of the Ball. It had been stressful to find her partner and deal with everything that night, but then after the fireworks when she was suddenly whisked into a marriage ceremony and then the fulfillment of that marriage.... She never wanted to talk about it, even if she had been able to.

But that strange winged man had talked to her Thomas and calmed him down. Brigittia had hugged her and calmed her down. Thank goodness they were so strong. Soon enough, Thomas had come back and took Brigid by the hand to plan their life forward. He said they could live on one of his family's estates and then choose where they really wanted to live together. Thomas already had colts he had been training and could start his own herd. It would just take a little time. They had time.

The dawn was gorgeous as Brigid and Thomas climbed into his carriage; hers having already been sent back to her parent's estate.

Gorgeous colors painted the sky, more beautiful than the fireworks the night before, and the morning air smelled fresh and clean. Brigid was tired, but she was happy leaving the ball with her fated mate. She fell asleep in the carriage, lulled to sleep by the sound of gravel under the wheels as she rested her head against Thomas' shoulder.

Brigid started awake, confused as she straightened up, until she looked down at her hand laced with Thomas' fingers. A smile played at her lips as she raised her free hand to her cheek, where the mask had been fused to her face just twelve hours earlier. So much had happened and so many dreams come true. Her smile grew as she looked down at the fated mate's tattoo inked on both their wrists. She was married to a beautiful, kind man who made her laugh. He was gentle and considerate too.

He said there was a cottage on the edge of his family's estate that they could move into right away. He wasn't sure if it was furnished, but that was easy to fix. It was close to her parents' home and Senator Vale would immediately send her daughter's dowry, wedding chests, and extravagant gifts. Brigid wasn't worried. Supper might be a challenge. She only knew the basics of cooking, as servants had always done the regular meals, but she would learn. Thomas said not to worry, so she didn't.

A frown creased her forehead as she thought about the wedding chests and gifts. Brigid worried that her mother might be upset that the wedding ceremony had already happened. Surely she would have wanted a big ceremony to shine on her political status.

"Thomas darling, do you think our families will be upset?"

"Hmm?" Thomas had been thinking deeply and had not realized that Brigid had woken up.

"Do you think our parents may be upset that we are married, and they weren't even invited?"

"Thank the gods!" exclaimed Thomas, thinking of the whole ceremony.

Brigid blushed, too. "No, not the actual ceremony, oh my! But I mean a wedding ceremony."

"Oh," Thomas realized that her mother probably would feel like she had missed an important event. "Oh, yes, they may be."

"What do we do?" whispered Brigid.

"I dunno. Do you think we could have another ceremony? Like one with our family and friends?"

"Oh! Yes, that's a good idea. That must happen all the time, don't you think? If these balls always end in marriages, but no one knows that? It must be that people do a second ceremony afterwards."

"Hmm, yeah." He pondered this for a minute. "You must be right. Your mom and my dad both probably have political people they want to invite. Shite, you need a ring, too."

"Oh!" Brigid had totally forgotten about an engagement ring. They hadn't ever been engaged, after all. "Well, these tattoos might cover that."

"Oh, yeah. That makes sense." He chuckled then. "Besides, I don't have a ring to give you right now."

"That's understandable." Brigid was practical, but still a small pang of jealousy wound through her. A ring would be nice.

Thomas wasn't a complete idiot and began pondering whether he could save up enough money to buy her a delightful piece of jewelry for their anniversary in a year. Nothing else about this was normal, so why give jewelry in the normal timeframe?

"My mom and your dad know each other, so that may be good."

"Uhhuh," Thomas wasn't certain, but he was pretty sure that his dad did not like the senator. Brigid seemed oblivious to that, so he wouldn't bring it up. "The bride's family usually plans the wedding, right? So your family will want to set that up? No, that sounded wrong. I'm not trying to dump it on you, but-"

"Relax. We've just been thrown into this, I get it."

They both untensed and relaxed a little. Then Brigid said, "We'll need to talk to our families, of course, but maybe that makes the most sense, to divide and conquer this. I kinda take over the wedding planning and you take over setting up our house. But we talk to each other, of course."

Thomas nodded. It made sense. "Yeah, ok. We'll continue on to this house right now so we can crash there and sleep in the guest beds for a few hours. Then, I guess, we will go to meet our families. Or did you want to send a message and have them both come to this house and we only have to go through everything once?"

"Huh. I hadn't thought of that, but yeah, once sounds way better. And if we send them a message now, with the invite for this afternoon because we need to rest, then they aren't worrying, but we can actually have some rest."

"Good, it's settled then. We'll send messages as soon as we arrive and find some paper to write a quick note to our parents."

Just then, the carriage dipped over a bump as it turned onto a gravel drive to their new home.

Chapter 22 - Aetherius

Around us were all sorts of muffled chaos. Overwhelmingly, it seemed, guests were not prepared and did not know about the marriage ceremony. At least we were only surprised by the need to be observed consummating it. Our observer was kind and gave us the illusion of space. I have no idea if the cabana was warded, so she could hear what we were saying, but at the very least, we went through the ceremony without force. By dawn, some of the other couples had less choice, it seemed.

Brigittia had startled me when she climbed on my lap, and I was embarrassed that I immediately grew hard under her. But she laughed at me and we grew easier with each other. We slowly began touching each other and actually talking to get to know one another. My hands felt so natural holding onto her waist. We both pretended that she didn't have silent tears as I softly kissed her.

The second time I kissed her, she kissed me back, her tongue darting out to tease my lips. I groaned, and she giggled.

"Since we're being so honest with each other," she began, "you should know that while I'm not really experienced in...this. I'm not a complete novice. It has been a part of my education, too."

"I can tell." I struggled to say.

"I guess I mean to say, you've been kind so far and I truly appreciate that, but you don't have to treat me with kid gloves."

"But you deserve to be treated well. You deserve kindness and care. Don't *ever* let anyone tell you differently." I pulled back to hold her stare. Her blue eyes were like deep crystal pools, so clear you couldn't be sure how deep they were, but it felt like you could fall into them forever.

"Ok," she said, but I hear the lack of conviction in her tone.

"I mean it. No matter what happens going forward between us, we need honesty and respect between us. And I will do everything I can to protect you always, for you to have what you deserve." I kissed her quickly again and whispered, "Remember, I am an Eudaemon, and we are the protectors"

She nodded and leaned forward to kiss me as she shifted her body backwards. She fumbled a little as she tried to undo my pants.

"Are you sure you're ready?" I held my hand over her fingers, forcing her to pause.

She didn't look at me, but I could see her cheeks redden again. "Yes, I think this part of the ceremony just hangs over us until we complete it. I feel like we need to just...do it, and then we can relax more."

She wasn't wrong, but it felt so forced. Truthfully, it was forced.

"Yeah," I sighed in agreement as I freed her hands. I unbuckled my belt and loosened my pants. "How do we do this so you're most comfortable?"

"Your wings can shield us some, I had said."

"You did, and when I am on top of you, I will do my best to shield us. But what I meant was, do you have a favored position or...Light, I don't even know what to ask. How do I make this easiest?"

She smiled in empathy at my frustration. "I don't know. Truly, I don't know how to answer that." Her fingers slipped into my pants and I groaned again, despite the unhappy wailing coming from nearby.

I lifted her off of me then and stood up to slip off my pants and loosen my shirt. While I was unbuttoning my collar, she moved up on her knees and began stroking me. I closed my eyes and enjoyed her talented fingers. My eyes popped open as I felt her mouth encircle my shaft. She flicked her tongue around the head and then slid me deeper in, pressing me against her tongue. She pulled her mouth off and licked down the length of me, from the bulging head to my balls, and gently sucked the vein as her mouth moved up again. I shivered and goose bumps covered me. I cupped my face against her cheek. The one that the mask had imprisoned for hours. "You don't have to do this."

"Let me," she said. "It helps me to relax into this."

"In that case, I'm not going to argue," I chuckled. "You are very talented." And I sucked in a breath in pleasure. I enjoyed it very much, as she played a little with tempo and angle to find what seemed to work best for both of us. But once she began cupping and gently tugging on my balls, I had to stop her.

"Hey now, you can't keep doing that." When she looked at me questioningly, I grinned, "I don't think your mouth will count as consummation, and that seems rude."

"Not rude, but no, probably not," she giggled.

"Your turn," I said. Apparently, it was the wrong suggestion. She immediately tensed up.

"No."

"No?"

"No, not here, not now, anyway. I just, I-" she huffed a breath. "Not now."

"Ok, I just wanted to be fair."

"Yeah, but we're good."

"Ok, here." I handed her the glass of water and sat down beside her. She sipped it obligingly, and I unbuttoned my shirt the rest of the way.

"I think," I said, "we could keep most of your clothes on for this, if that will help."

She flashed a grateful grin at me. "I appreciate that. Thank you." She leaned forward and ran a hand down my chest, grazing her fingers against my manhood, making it quiver with anticipation. "But that also seems cumbersome and rather unfair. I have a layer under this. Perhaps that would work."

She stood up then and began trying to unlace the back of her dress.

I stood up and held my wings out around us as I stepped behind her and moved her so she was protected from the prying eyes of our watcher. When the laces were loosened, she pulled down on her sleeve, baring her shoulder. I began to kiss her neck, and I felt her shiver, but from the heat radiating off her skin, I knew she wasn't cold. She tilted her head, showing her neck and shoulder vulnerable to me. Together, we tugged her dress down until it slipped off over her hips and to the floor. The thin silk she had left was cool and slippery and easily let me feel her feverish body. She lifted my hand up to cup her breast through the thin fabric and turned to match her lips to mine. I slid my other hand down to her ass and then lifted her leg up and around mine. I let my wing drop a little so our watcher could see, but the heat between her legs was calling to me and I could hardly go slow.

"The bed," she whispered.

I immediately picked her up. She wrapped both legs around me and we basically fell onto the bed. She kept her legs around me, but loosened her grip as I held myself above her, teasing against her heat."

"Please," she said.

I didn't mean to make her beg. I just wanted her to be ready. The last thing I want to do is cause her pain. "Are you sure?" She nodded and arched up as her hands firmly grasped me.

"I'm sure." She held me and slid the tip of my cock against her clit. I nearly came just from the wet heat she offered. Then she gently slid me down so I could push in.

I lost all sense of time or anything more than our bodies moving against each other, and barely pulling back to arc against each other again. I could see her nipples harden through the thin material and held my palm against her breast. The heat of my hand momentarily softening it, and then her nipple peaked again, as her breathing hitched and her eyes widened. I grinned and kissed her hard. She growled into my throat and kissed me back just as hard. A few more thrusts and I came just as powerfully and with a growl of my own. Panting, we lay there a moment, sweat slick between us, my weight held up on my elbows and knees, her hands tracing little circles on the side of my ribs.

After a moment, I scooted back and made sure she was decently covered, then I rolled off of her onto the open space of the bed. She poured some fresh water into the glass and handed it to me, and sipped from the other herself. My satisfied smirk returned as soon as I gulped down my water and flopped back.

"Is she still there?" I asked without opening my eyes again.

"Who?"

"Our watcher?" I felt Brigittia sit up a little beside me.

"Oh, no, I don't see her. Others are still stationed in front of other cabanas, but not so many now. And ew, I can see inside that cabana. I'm done looking."

I laughed deep in my throat. Clearly this girl wasn't a prude, but we all have our distastes. We both shifted so we were sitting up against the pillows, and Brigittia pulled a blanket up over her legs.

"Cold?" I asked.

"Not exactly, but not not-cold either."

"Hmm." I was desperately trying to think of something not awkward to say when she laughed again.

"This is almost worse, isn't it?" she asked. "Like, I thought that would be the most awkward thing ever tonight, and now any conversation seems completely inane."

"It does," I laughed too. "I was thinking the same."

"At least we both seemed to enjoy it-"

"Oh, I did!"

"Good, because that would be even more embarrassing and awkward if one of us didn't."

"Uhhuh," I agreed. "I wonder if they'll bring more food and drinks."

"I wonder if we have to stay here or if we can wander around. I feel like it might be easier to talk if we could walk through the gardens or something. Like talking and looking at the stars would be easier than staring into the eyes of a stranger I just fucked."

I'm telling you, this girl is perfect.

"Hand me my pants and I'll have a look around, if you want."

"Would you?"

"Seems like the least I could do right now."

She smiled gratefully, and my heart melted a little.

This ball did not go as planned for the romantic in me. But I have achieved the goal of a mate, and an intelligent, humorous, and courageous one at that. We can be friends, and friends with benefits as she gives me the heirs I so desperately need. We'll see what I can offer her beyond protections, and the freedom to be with the one she truly loves in every way except legal marriage. She and I are married, but that doesn't mean we have to have a typical unhappy marriage.

I had hoped to have someone to wander the world with. And we could, except that any blind fool can see that she is in love with the horse-boy. I am neither blind nor a fool. He appears to be just as love-struck by her as that other girl is of him. What drama these mortals create! Though a part of me will always blame these ball organizers, too. Had there not been such a desire for stupid riddles, I could have met my date before or at least reached out, so we found each other right away and she never even fell for him. Or, those fate sisters are just cackling their heads off at the great joke they played upon me. That is possible too. Retaliation for when my kitten played with their balls of yarn. Damn women, they complicate my life.

We finished the Quinquennial Masquerade Ball as friends. Brigittia and I were awkward but friendly. That may sum up the rest of our lives, I think. We were eventually fed again, or at least buffets and music were provided, and we were allowed to walk the grounds once each couple's watcher gave the ok. I never saw the woman again who had been set to watch us, but apparently she checked all the boxes that we had consummated our vows. Brigittia and I were free to wander the grounds as we wished. We saw other couples prevented from leaving the grounds quite forcibly, and we didn't even make an attempt.

Just as dawn was breaking, that dark-haired girl with the white streak came barreling over to us and sobbed in Brigittia's arms. Brigittia looked as surprised as I felt until we saw that horse-boy Thomas walking over morosely. He lit up a little, seeing Brigittia, and then looked even more morose, like an abused puppy. Brigittia, on the other hand, shot up so many wards about herself that goosebumps rose on my skin immediately and I wasn't even touching her. It was the one time this evening that I saw her, completely unsure what to do. Apparently, she and Brigid were friends from youth, but Brigittia was clearly struggling between being loyal to me and our vows versus what her heart so obviously yearned for - horse-boy.

I had to hold back and let them walk ahead for a moment. I had found the perfect partner, and she was willing to fulfill her responsibilities and vows, but clearly she felt something much deeper for horse-boy. Her eyes burned for him, even as she turned away to comfort her friend. I could feel the emotions roiling around her, and I was rather surprised that actual storm clouds didn't roll in with all the energy swirling about her. She was powerful!

I snarled and raged internally for a few minutes, and then a plan began to form. I gave her a few more minutes to comfort her friend, and for that electrifying energy to calm a little, too. The centuries had taught me patience. Then I altered my course to walk beside the horse-boy.

"Oh, hi," he said when he noticed me walking beside me. He smelled apprehensive.

I snorted a laugh and then said, "Listen, we have a few issues to work out, but we can make both ladies happy. That's our duty."

He looked at me with obvious mixed feelings of hope and hopelessness. "How?"

"I have an idea, but we have to convince them as well." He nodded, and I went on, "Between her magic and her fae blood, Brigittia will live longer than you or the dark-haired girl."

"Brigid is fae too. Well, partly fae."

"But does she have magic like Brigittia?"

"Brigittia has magic?"

Well, shite. "Yes, yes, she does. And it will add to her lifespan."

"Huh?"

"Nevermind," I sighed heavily. "Here's my idea: you and Brigid are married. You live happily ever after with your wife. Brigittia and I will have a home somewhere. You can come visit her as often as you wish, until your wife dies, and then you can spend more time with the longer-living Brigittia."

Horse-boy blinked at me as the idea began to settle over him. Now, to be fair, I was conveniently leaving out the part that his half-centaur and half mortal life span would be the same as Brigid's, not Brigittia's, but why quibble over numbers? I was giving him an out that helped his heart and met his responsibilities.

"I'm, I'm not sure I quite understand."

Oh, I believe that. But surely you have heard of polyamory? "You can follow your heart and meet your responsibilities while also letting that poor girl, Brigid, have what her heart desires. You and Brigittia may not have the perfect life, but you can still have each other some of the time."

"But what about you?"

"I'll manage. I need Brigittia to bear me an heir, but if her heart yearns for you, she can never be truly mine."

"Oh."

"Think about it. Go comfort your wife."

"My wi-" He huffed. "Yes. Thank you."

We walked over to the ladies. I let my wing brush up against Brigitta and felt a shock of electricity that almost brought me to my knees. Light, she was strong! Horse-boy walked up and took Brigid's hand.

"Let's walk and talk a minute. I think I have an idea for us all to be happy." Brigittia looked at me with hope and concern in her eyes.

Chapter 23 - Brigittia

Aetherius had sent his carriage away during the night, or maybe right after he arrived, Brigittia wasn't sure. So they rode together in her carriage to the Lunaire estate. It seemed right that Brigittia's parents should meet her husband, and he fully supported it.

Riding together in the carriage in a comfortable silence, Brigittia reflected on the Ball and all that handled up to it.

"I didn't even want to come, y'know that?" she blurted.

"Hmm, I could see that. Which is why you so carefully researched it, to know what you were getting into."

"Well, most of it anyway," chuckled Brigittia, her cheeks reddening.

Aetherius chuckled, "Alright, you were more prepared than most."

"Uhhuh. I knew the ball was less about fun and food and more about political alliances. I just didn't realize that those alliances were so publicly proven."

"Nor did I," admitted Aetherius. "Unlike you, I chose to attend the ball. My people have long had a dwindling bloodline, and we agreed that we needed to strengthen it."

"So all you wanted was a mate to bear you children?" irritation flashed through Brigittia.

"No, that's not all I wanted." Aetherius spoke softly, and the flames of anger in Brigittia banked. "No, I need a mate to strengthen my bloodline. I *want* a lover and a friend in my mate. I want someone to spend my days with and my nights. I want a partner."

Brigittia looked at him sorrowfully. "I swear I can be a partner and a friend. I can bear you children that we raise. But I don't know if I can love you."

Aetherius dipped his head. "I know. But as I said at the ball, we can find an arrangement that suits us all, if you're willing."

"Polyamory?"

"Yes."

"Maybe. It's not what I ever dreamed of."

"No. I imagine this wasn't the wedding of your dreams, either."

Brigittia scoffed, "No."

"We'll have to see then what dreams of yours I can make true."

Brigittia smiled. This ball, this wedding, certainly the ceremony, was unlike anything she had imagined. But Aetherius seemed kind, intelligent, and willing to listen to her. He was comfortable, Brigittia suddenly realized. Partners and friends might be better than suddenly falling in, and later out, of love.

Aetherius had time, so he let her think. The silence was comfortable, and they were both exhausted. Another mile or so later, he cleared his throat and suggested, "As much as we both seem to enjoy the quiet, perhaps we should have a plan that we can share with your parents."

"Indeed." She smiled ruefully. "I don't think this is quite what they expected. And while they will not think less of you for your wings, the whole demon thing might give them hesitation."

"Does no one learn about Eudaemons anymore?" asked Aetherius with mock frustration.

"I mean, honestly?"

"Of course. Always."

"Hmm, then honestly I think I might have heard of demons that were good, not evil, but..." she trailed off.

"Yeah. Ok." He paused, "but if they are as educated as you, we can explain, and they can later do more research."

Brigittia was nodding. "Yes, and we can ask for my tutor to pull some research from the library for them. They will listen to us and be willing to learn. Still, I think your wings and story may take them a...moment to adjust to. Along with the unexpected marriage, well, we should cut them some slack."

"I can be very charming." He winked, "Devilishly so."

Brigittia threw her head back and laughed. The exhaustion, the stress, and the absolute absurdity of it all landed on her and her laughter took over, devolving into tears with the laughter. At first, Aetherius was concerned that he had truly upset her, but then she set a hand on his thigh. A little warmth sank into his skin and, with it, a tiny opening into her emotions. Clearly, she was letting him in through her walls and wards. Relieved, he realized that while she might have a tinge of hysteria; it was from exhaustion, not fear, and she was truly laughing. Aetherius relaxed and grinned.

After a few moments, Brigittia calmed into giggles and began wiping the tears from her eyes. "Sorry," she said.

"No, I think you're allowed to be a bit unhinged for a few moments. I've got you. I mean-" He paused suddenly, realizing how possessive that sounded and not at all his intent.

"Shh, I get it. You've got my back."

"Yeah. I will never own you. Never."

"Nope. You won't." She flashed a feral grin at him.

"Right." He smiled back and then said, "Thank you."

"For what?"

"Letting me in."

"Oh. Yeah. I'll need some practice at that. I'm used to keeping everyone out."

Interesting, he wondered why she felt the need to wall herself up all the time. "Right, we have time. For that, at least. But I think we're approaching your family's estate, so maybe we should have a rough plan."

Brigittia glanced out the window and nodded. Then started, when she processed that he knew where her family's estate was.

"I knew you were my partner, remember?" He asked softly. Then, with more energy, he said, "Now, let's decide where we shall live. Or, where you should live and I to visit, if you prefer."

And so their new roles and new lives began. As expected, the political party was thrown by Senator Vale and Councilor Briarthorne in the shape of a wedding reception. The word was the family had kept the actual ceremony small.

The Lunaire family simply put out that they had chosen a secret ceremony to be kept private, but they wanted everyone to join the party. Unquestionably, Brigitte and Aetherius had more fun at their party. The music was better, too.

Whether there was residual magic at play or it was just the summer air, the people didn't seem to note that there were an awful lot of private marriages happening. Soon it was forgotten that the engagement periods had been nonexistent. Like the humans, the wolves took it all in stride, and both Brigid and Brigitte's pets were happy in their new homes. Although the horses were less fond of Skye than Thomas might have wished. Zara sniffed Aetherius' wings with great curiosity and then accepted him as easily as her mistress.

The year passed uneventfully. Brigid had a happy home with Thomas and they expected several bouncing, gurgling babies that soon would grow into playful toddlers, then young children. Unfortunately, despite his family's health, their herd of horses did not grow as well. Thomas began traveling to find new horse bloodlines. Brigid wasn't happy that he put himself in danger, but she supported the plan for Thomas to improve their herd. It was clearly the right thing to do.

Aetherius and Brigittia lived a quite unconventional life. They soon found a cottage that they both liked high up on the cliffs by the ocean, with a deep forest behind it. A beautiful stone wall was set back in the woods and harbored gorgeous creeping flowers. They spent a year getting to know each other and traveling on brief trips around the continent. As they traveled, Aetherius taught Brigittia to fuel her power more and more from the energies of the earth, wind, sun, and stars. But where she truly felt at peace was on or near the ocean.

"It's the one thing more powerful than you can ever be," said Aetherius. "Thus, you feel safe near it."

They spent a little over a year traveling around and then finding the perfect cottage for a forever home. Every day was spent with time to read and to chat. But finally, Aetherius said over breakfast, "As much as I have enjoyed this year of rest and adventures with you, Bri, I feel stirrings that I am neglecting my duties."

"Have you?" Brigitte looked up from her mending. "That must feel frustrating."

"Hmm, it's not as severe as that yet, but I imagine it will be."

"So now what then? Where do we go?"

"You, my dear, don't go anywhere," he paused, "unless you're uncomfortable staying here without me."

"I'm not afraid, no." She was confused, so she sat back, waiting for more information. She trusted him.

"I have familial duties. In essence, I have taken a vacation, but I need to right some wrongs and go back to work." Aetherius answered with a grin, but the seriousness was underneath it.

"So you travel off alone, saving the world, and I stay here doing my thing."

"Well, not so much saving the world, but yes." He tilted his head, watching her. "You knew this would come, yeah?"

"Yes," said Brigittia slowly. "But I'm going to miss you."

"Gee thanks," he said dryly.

"No, I mean, well yes." Brigittia smiled ruefully. "When we were first married, we talked about it as an arranged marriage and we would work to become friends, but we didn't expect to fall in love. And we have become friends. I enjoy being with you. It will be strange to spend my days alone again."

"Do you wish we could change this? Go back in time as it were, so you could be with him?"

"I don't know." Brigittia chewed her lip. "I still have this image of him as beautiful and amazing, but in a few hours I never really got to know him, y'know. I have no idea if he actually is as appealing as I remember. But I know you. I'm happy with our time together."

Aetherius nodded. Brigittia didn't need a lecture and he couldn't add anything of value to her thoughts. Horse-boy would always be a shadow in their lives, but he wasn't afraid of shadows.

"You'll be able to contact me, always. My family will be around, too, if you should need something."

"Mmhmm."

"I think you like me, Brigittia."

"Of course."

"No, I mean you *like* like me," he grinned.

Brigittia laughed, "Oh." She set down her mending then and moved over to straddle his lap. "Maybe. Do you like me, too?"

"You have no idea how much," he groaned. Aetherius leaned his forehead against hers. "I thought, a year ago, that you and I would spend a few weeks getting to know each other, then we would find you a cottage where you could live comfortably and you would meet your duties while pining for Horse-boy."

"Horse-boy?" Brigittia snorted.

"Sorry. That's how I think of him. The nickname sorta popped into my head at the ball and stuck."

"What nickname do you have for me?" She pulled back to look at his face.

He grinned. "Spitfire, most of the time."

"Most of the time?"

"Yeah." Aetherius smiled and leaned forward, kissing her lips.

Brigittia laughed softly and as she did, her lips parted and their kiss deepened. She flicked out her tongue, teasing his lips. Aetherius groaned and pulled her closer against him.

"Maybe we should go upstairs?"

"Yeah?"

Brigittia bit her lip again, uncharacteristically shy. "Yeah."

They had been intimate a few times through the year, but more as a friends-with-benefits type of feeling. This time, she wanted to have the closeness, too. She let her aura encompass him then, the heat of her feelings and her desire.

Aetherius sucked in his breath as her energy enveloped him. He didn't say a word, but scooped Brigittia up, wings wrapped around her, and brought them upstairs.

Chapter 24 - Routines settled

"You're sure you're set then?" Thomas asked Brigid that morning as he prepared to leave. After a year of marriage, they had quite a comfortable life and routine. Brigid had settled into doing charity work under her mother's office - Senator Vale loved to say she supported the working people, and Thomas was building up his herd.

"Of course, silly!" Brigid flashed her husband a bright smile. "This dinner my mother is throwing will go quite late, and then tomorrow I am at the library most of the day working with those students. I'll hardly even know you're gone."

Still, Thomas hesitated. His wife was smart and capable, but still he worried. The fact that she was pregnant with their first child just made him more nervous.

"Seriously, Thomas, I'll be fine. We've arranged a carriage to drive me to and from the dinner, so I don't even have to do anything with that or when I come home to care for the horses. Skye will protect me here better than most men."

Skye pricked her ears when she heard her name, and gave a wolfish smile, tongue lolling out of her mouth.

Thomas gave Skye a quick scratch behind the ear. "Yes, you do. You'll be fine. I just worry, y'know."

"I do know," said Brigid softly. "It's no different from how I worry about you when you travel."

"Eh, I'll be fine," Thomas shook his head. "I've made this trip at least a hundred times. I'll be home before you know it with more colts."

"Alright," Brigid leaned in to kiss him. "Bring me home a pretty one."

"I'll try, but that's not my usual criteria." Thomas grinned at her.

Brigid grinned too. "Maybe it should be."

"Right." Thomas hauled himself up on his horse then and waved. "I should be home late tomorrow, but maybe the next morning if the colts travel slowly."

"Yeah, be safe. I'll see you soon." Brigid shaded her eyes against the morning sun as he rode off. She loved spending time with her husband, but she wasn't at all opposed to spending a quiet morning with just her wolf for company along with a good book and cafe.

That evening, the dinner party was elegant and fun. Unlike the first formal dinner Brigid had attended after the ball, this one had no incense. Smelling the incense at that dinner had nearly sent her into a reeling panic attack. Luckily, Thomas had immediately understood and made an excuse for them to step outside. Truthfully, he appreciated the fresh air as well.

Tonight, Brigid sat at her mother's table with her cousin, Titania.

"These are delicious!" exclaimed Brigid. "We eat a lot of salads, but I never thought to add berries to them." She popped another grape into her mouth, enjoying the splash of sweetness across her tongue.

"No?" asked Titania. "I love adding strawberries to mine, especially if some greens are more bitter. It adds a lovely contrast."

"Mm-hmm. I have blackberries growing behind our cottage. I think I will try it with those. Especially as the dandy lion greens have gotten quite tart, as you say."

"The wine helps too," giggled Titania.

"I enjoy a good vintage. And this is an excellent vintage." Brigid softly clinked her glass against her cousins and they shared a grin, remembering the time they had snuck into the wine cellar when they were much younger. They had sampled several excellent vintages that day. Until they were caught.

"Ladies!" hissed Senator Vale. Apparently, they were not being proper enough.

"Yes, mother. Sorry." Brigid carefully avoided looking at Titania.

Thomas was enjoying his alcohol, too. But his was foamy and full of hops. The people surrounding Thomas in the tavern were boisterous, and definitely would not be approved of by Senator Vale. Thomas was relaxed. He was more than content to stay home training horses and spending time with his wife, but it was nice to get out and share jokes with other travelers, share stories of obvious exaggeration, and fart when he felt like it. Married life had its perks, but so did a single life. Often he traveled with his best friend, Alderic, but on this trip he was alone. A buxom barmaid came over to sit on his lap like she had done tens of times before.

"Ahh, no, lass. I'm married now."

"Are you?" She arched an eyebrow. "I don't see her. I don't think I believe you."

"No, I am truly married and boring now."

"Just because you're married doesn't mean you need to be boring."

"Maybe not, but this," Thomas indicated his wrist, "leads me to faithful."

The barmaid's eyes widened when she saw the fated mate's tattoo. "Fine then," she playfully pouted. "But if you change your mind..."

"Aye lass, I appreciate it."

"Mm-hmm. I'll bring you a mug. My wedding gift for you." She slipped off his lap regretfully and soon came back with a large mug filled to the brim with golden liquid and white foam.

A couple more hopeful barmaids tried their luck with Thomas, but none succeeded.

Brigid never had that same problem. It was understood that she couldn't be approached when she was the senator's daughter. Now that she was married, she didn't even get the flirty eye contact. Not that she wanted it particularly. Thomas made her completely happy at home, and she taught several groups of young ladies many life skills from political negotiations to sewing and mending, wine tasting to stashing weapons in hairstyles. Still, a few flirty eyes would give a nice boost to her day. Especially when she felt a little like a pregnant cow right now.

Thomas and Brigid might have a life of domestic bliss, but Brigittia was just coming into a whole new life. While it was never made much of, she was an heir apparent for her country, but unless her brother and sister are first killed, she's third in line and unlikely to ever seat the throne. She is important politically until she marries Aetherius and drops away from society. Brigittia never had any desire to rule, but it's why her education was more complete.

Now she puts to use her self-sufficiency skills, hunting, trapping, and fishing her meat, while foraging berries, seaweed, and various plants. Her gardens, herbs and vegetables kept her happy through the spring and summer. Just like her grandmother's house, a haven for her when she was younger, she soon has flowers in all the windows, and bunches of herbs hung and drying from the ceiling all over. She had little sachets of herbs and flowers tucked into her closet to keep the clothes fresh, and others under her pillows to help her sleep. She created and sampled many blends for teas, and had many tinctures in the cupboards, resting and becoming more potent. She always had a pan of sea water by the hearth for the water to evaporate and the minerals left behind to season her foods. Brigittia had her own form of domestic bliss. Except for the yearning.

There was this feeling that kept her restless through her restful days and her busy days. It was like a task that she still needed to do, but she couldn't remember what. It nagged her less when she walked the cliffs and watched out to see or deep in the woods listening to the sounds of undisturbed nature. She felt like the trees were trying to whisper to her and give her a hint, but she couldn't quite hear.

The weeks passed. Then the months passed. And years passed. Aetherius came and went, staying a few hours or a few weeks at a time. They were content together, but Aetherius noticed a change in her. At the ball and the year after, Brigittia had been a strong, young woman, filled with responsibility and awareness. Now she was a strong woman. She was nothing like a young woman any longer. She had moved in form from maid to matron.

Around the same time, Aetherius began hearing rumors of a witch woman living in the woods. With a chuckle, he realized they were talking about his wife. Someone had seen her foraging and then not seen any hint of her again. Another had heard her talking with Zara, and Zara obviously enthralled with her. She would be amused to be considered a witchy woman.

But upon a conversation with his brother, he realized that maybe there was more to it.

"You always have the luck, Aetherius. Your cottage is smack in the center of the unusual calm."

"What do you mean?"

"Have you not noticed? It's the one area of the continent that has not had these strange electric storms, and forest fires, and upheaval."

"What do you mean?"

"Hmm, my wise brother, you didn't choose it on purpose? Actually, it may only be since you did move in. But everywhere else seems to have tragedies and chaos, except the area near your cottage."

"But why?"

"Wouldn't we like to know."

Aetherius relaxed the crease that was forming in his forehead, then asked, "And what is this about the ley lines shifting?"

"Aye, that's what they're saying. Ley lines are always like rivers and gradually shift, but now several are shifting much faster and slowly shifting towards that same area."

"Auld magic?"

"We don't know."

"So the auld magic is shifting and my wife is being accused of being a witch." He tapped his thumb against his thigh while thinking.

"Is she? A witch, I mean."

"I didn't think so, but...she mentioned that her ancestry is that of Avalon. And she has energies and wards I have never felt before."

"The Isles?"

"Yeah."

"Go home, brother. Protect her. None of the witches of Avalon have been here for a very long time. If their magic is coming alive in her, she needs a teacher."

"I can't teach her how to wield those powers."

"No, but you protect her until I find a crone to send."

Aetherius nodded in agreement. They hugged goodbye and hurried their own ways.

Aetherius felt it as soon as he landed in the yard of the cottage. The air was saltier than he remembered; the trees were larger than he remembered, and the garden was lush. Then he saw her standing at the cliff.

There was no breeze on his skin, but standing there, fifty paces from him, the wind whipped Brigittia's hair. The waves thundered and crashed out of sight below her. Zale sensed his arrival and looked back at him. Her tail thumped, but she didn't leave her mistress' side. Suddenly, a shaft of sunlight broke through the clouds and lit up Brigittia's auburn hair so it looked like flames dancing around her head.

Aetherius sucked in a breath. She looked like a goddess. Feeling the energy rolling off of her and through the ground and air surrounding him, he believed it. She could be a lost goddess, come back to earth to revitalize the ladies of Avalon. She was amazing. She was his wife. Aetherius grinned. She was beautifully perfect and his partner.

Brigittia turned then and her eyes shone when she saw him as she smiled.

Brigittia

Zara felt Aetherius arrive at our cottage before me. I was looking out over the ocean like I'm drawn to do so often. Her tail started thumping, and that only happened for him and I. The way he looked at me was different, like he was in awe of me. Not in an "aww you look sexy today," kind of way, but like he was seeing this fresh energy that I feel. *Could he see it?*

We made love that night like we never had before. With every interaction, he was respectful and treated me like an equal before, but now I *felt* like an equal. Not just capable, but an equal. I no longer felt the distance of his centuries between us. *What has changed?*

"So you're the scary witch, huh?" Aetherius asked me over breakfast.

"Huh?" I was completely confused.

"My brother was telling me, and then I listened around. You're beginning to have a reputation."

"What are you talking about?"

He chuckled. "Apparently people have seen you, 'a wild woman,' gathering herbs and staring off the cliffs and they have decided that you're a witch."

I scoffed at the ridiculousness of this, but then he continued more seriously.

"You might be."

"Might be what?"

"You might be a witch. When I got here last night and the wind was whipping your hair, you certainly looked like a goddess. With your Avalonian blood, it wouldn't be far-fetched."

I raised an eyebrow at him, but at the same time, it clicked. I chewed my lip for a minute and tucked my hair behind an ear as I thought about it. He let me have the quiet and think.

"What would it feel like if I were?"

He blinked fast. "I'm, umm, I'm not sure. Not being a witch and all." He tapped a finger against his leg while he contemplated the question. "I know you feel the Ley lines. Hey, by the way, those are apparently moving, too."

"Huh? They always move."

"No. I mean, well, yes. They always flow like water, and very slowly they change course. Like over thousands of years, they shift. But now they are noticeably shifting closer to here."

"Here?!"

"Uhhuh," he nodded, calm despite my ill ease.

"What does that mean?"

"I'm not sure, but I think it's like calling like. I think your energy is drawing that energy. Just like you're drawn to lightning storms and the ocean. Like to like."

My turn to blink fast as I tried to understand. I played with a strand of hair, wrapping it around my finger and pulling my finger through and then wrapping it again.

"Is that bad?"

"I don't think it's necessarily bad, but it is...unusual." He was quiet for a moment and then continued, "I don't want you to be scared of this. We just don't understand it."

"We?"

"Me, you, my brother, who mentioned it to me." He paused for a moment, then continued, "He was going to try to find someone who might guide you. I can show you how to search out energies. You already mastered that. And you figured out how to use those natural energies to fuel your wards and such, but I don't know anything else to help you. There aren't any priestesses of Avalon anymore, but he's searching for someone who might have knowledge who can help."

"What does this make me?" I asked quietly.

"What do you want it to mean?" he asked.

"I don't know." I pulled and wrapped my hair some more. "I didn't look for this or ask for it. What do I do with it?"

"It's not a bad feeling, is it? It's not trying to control you, right?"

"No!" I shook my head vigorously. I wasn't afraid or feeling controlled.

"Then you get to choose how to use it." He tilted his head. "When I got here, you were looking out over the water. What were you looking at?'

"I wasn't looking at anything. But it was like, like," I bit my lip as I tried to put the feeling into words. "It's like I'm searching and watching for something. Like I'm on guard. But I have no idea what I would be guarding against."

He nodded. "In many stories, the Avalonians were protectors of the realm. This may be why we are fated mates. We're both protectors."

I held his eyes. They held no fear, just curiosity. That felt right. I had never known my role. I had been an excellent scholar, but that's not really a job. I'm third in line for a crown that I never want to have, so my purpose has been vague. But a protector, the idea settles on me like a warm cloak on a fall day. It feels right.

"Maybe."

"Hmm. We don't need to decide right now." He flashed his gorgeous smile at me, then he stood and reached out a hand. "C'mon, let's go for a walk."

"A walk?"

"Sure, something. Let's move and do something, not stew about what we don't understand."

"Alright. Let me grab a basket." Seeing his confused look, I explained, "You never know what we might find. Berries, herbs, flowers, who knows?"

He laughed then. You really are a witch."

"I'm practical. Nothing witchy about it."

"Uhhuh." He grinned and took the basket from me.

Zara bounded ahead with her wolfish grin.

Chapter 25 - Brigittia and Thomas

Thomas began traveling further and farther to find additional sources of horses. On one such trip, a terrible storm forced him off the road and into the forest for shelter from the downpours. By the afternoon he was disoriented with the rain and wind and he feared he was going in circles. Thomas and his horse plodded on deeper into the trees to try to find a cave or some sort of shelter. Suddenly, the ground below his feet gave way. The horse whinnied in fright and they both went sliding and crashing down a bank they hadn't even sensed. As soon as they stopped tumbling, the horse snorted in disgust, her sides heaving with heavy breathing.

"I agree, Lady. I agree," said Thomas, laying a hand on her while he lay still, breathing hard. Then, he sat up and began running his hands up the mare's legs, checking for injuries. He let out a whoosh of breath when she seemed unhurt except for a few scratches. Thomas went to stand up himself and urge her up, but as soon as he started to stand and put weight on his left foot, he winced and cried out in pain. He became aware then of the light throbbing in his ankle and burning on his calf. "Well shite, Lady. I seem to be hurt myself."

Patiently, she rolled up onto her feet and then stood solidly beside him. Gratefully, he pulled himself up, using her stirrup. He patted her flank as he gingerly put weight on his foot again. Burning, white hot pain exploded out from his ankle. Looking down, he saw blood soaking through his pant leg. He leaned down to look more closely at his leg. The world spun, and he grabbed the stirrup again to steady himself. Lady huffed some air as if to ask him what he was doing. Thomas gripped the stirrup with one hand and put his palm against her hot flesh to ground himself, leaning his forehead against her shoulder.

She smelled like horse sweat and hay, comfortable and stable. Thomas breathed in deep again and then opened his eyes. Grimacing, he took another breath and reached up to pull himself into the saddle. Luckily, he could swing his leg over her back normally, but pain inflamed his entire leg as he held his foot in the stirrup against her.

"Well, this is gonna suck for both of us, I think." He clicked his tongue for Lady to begin walking forward. "I can't post today and likely will feel like a sack of potatoes on your back. Sorry, m'girl."

They plodded through the rain until they found an enormous bunch of evergreen trees that blocked most of the rain. The ground was almost dry under the heavy branches. Thomas stiffly slid down, keeping most of his weight on his right leg. The ankle was less sore now, just a dull beat echoing his heartbeat. But his calf was throbbing in counterpoint. The pant leg had crusted to the wound, but as he moved, unsaddling Lady and rubbing her down as best he could, the material pulled free and blood was soon trickling down his leg and again soaking his blood-crusted sock. Together, they spent a chilly night in the rain.

The next morning, Thomas saddled Lady and then hobbled after her as she searched out the water. She had always scented out good water, and her body language said it was close. Thomas thought his limping walk would be easier than climbing up and then sliding off her back again. She whickered with pleasure and picked up her pace. Thomas heard the stream then, so he patted her rump and let her go ahead. Suddenly, he caught his toe and fell forward into a stagnant pool of water. Immediately, a smell of sulfur clouded around Thomas as he tried to scoot back and get out of the water. Looking down, he was dismayed to see both legs covered with sticky, greenish mud. He stumbled back to his feet and caught up to Lady. He sat in the cold water below her and let the running water to wash his legs while he leaned upstream, cupping his hands full of cold water to gulp. Once he wasn't thirsty anymore, he tried rubbing and swirling his pant legs in the water, but not all the mud would release. Wincing with the movement and the cold water, Thomas stood back up, grabbing Lady's mane to steady himself. "Sorry, girl." Hurting a horse was the last thing he wanted to do, but luckily he had grabbed a full handful, so maybe it wasn't so bad. Lady stood stoic and still.

He moved stiffly to her other side and on the second try managed to swing up onto the saddle. Trying to cheer himself up, he noted that it wasn't raining anymore and the branches would likely dry soon in the sunlight.

Thomas hunched over the saddle and let Lady lead. She likely had a better idea than he did of where the road was. He was, admittedly, lost. He was also miserable. By afternoon, he knew he had a fever, and it was questionable which hurt more his head or his leg. He could hardly keep his eyes open. Lady's gait had changed, as she was aware of her rider not feeling right on her back.

Thomas was vaguely aware of it getting darker through his fuzzy vision. He was less aware of sliding off Lady and her hot breath as she nuzzled him on the ground.

Later, Thomas was sure he was dreaming as he felt himself rolled onto something sledlike, and then bumping over the ground. Every bump led to an echoing pounding in his skull. He thought he felt Lady's hot breath again and smelled hay, while she snorted her enjoyment at a rubdown. Which didn't make any sense. HIs hands, even his eyelids, were too heavy for him to move. But she snorted again. Then he felt straps under his shoulders and around his chest as he was again dragged, this time into warm and dark.

Thomas became aware of indoor sounds next. There was the sound of a crackling fire and a cat purring. Dishes were being washed quietly not too far away and there was an aroma of soup.

"Ahh, good, you're awake. I'm tempted to bring your horse in so she can see. She's worried about you, too."

Thomas cracked a weak smile. "Lady," he croaked. A cup was set against his lips and he sipped some cool water. It cut down his throat, but then he realized he was parched. He greedily tried to gulp some more."

"Easy now, or you'll vomit and neither of us wants that. I'll give you more in a moment." It was a calming voice hushing him. Thomas cracked an eye, but the light was painfully bright and he clamped his eyes shut again. He tried speaking again, and his voice was looser. "Lady," he whispered. "Her name is Lady, and she's a sweetheart."

"Yes, she is," the calm voice replied. "Well, Lady is wiped down, her feet cleaned, and she has water and some hay in my shed. There's room enough to lie down if she wishes, but not much else until it stops raining.

Thomas nodded, "Thanks."

"Hush, I didn't do it for you. But what I did for both of you was bring in the saddle and blanket. Those are drying by my fire."

Thomas nodded again and fell back asleep, vaguely aware of water dribbling between his lips.

Brigitte

I stood at my normal perch on the cliffs. Zara sniffed around and startled a rabbit, which she gleefully chased until it ducked down a hole. Then she happily began digging after it without a scarce chance of catching it. Nonetheless, she was happy and I could think.

While he hadn't recognized me, delirious as he was, I recognised Thomas immediately when Zara led me to him. His horse was a sweetheart and apparently was used to Skye, for she didn't really mind Zara. She willingly pulled the skid when I managed to roll Thomas onto it and hauled him back to the cottage. I don't know how long she had stood by him, but she was stiff and shivering when we came upon her. She had limbered up by the time she got to my cottage. I felt terrible for her, but appreciated her loyalty. I stripped off the saddle and blanket right away and covered her with a dry blanket when I went to fetch her some water. After she drank some, I struggled to drag Thomas into the cottage and set him near the fire to warm up as well. I stripped off his wet clothes and covered him with a dry blanket, too. Then I headed back out and led the sweet mare into the shed. I managed to rub her down, drying her completely. Then I found her some hay while I cleaned out her hooves. She had some nasty clay in them, but was a gentle soul while I cared for her. I thought of giving her some warm mash, but I wasn't sure how much would be too much and how little would be just a tease. So a bit of hay and fresh water and I let her be. She tried to follow me right back out, though. She was quite determined, clearly loyal to Thomas.

Back in my cottage, without the mare, Zara and I laid out the wet tack to dry and then we began cleaning up Thomas. I decided Brigid didn't need to know this. I didn't think my friend would appreciate me seeing her naked husband. He slept through our ministrations until I got to his leg. It was hot to the touch and dark red, clearly infected. So we set a warm poultice on it first for a bit to draw the poisons to the surface. Then I lanced it and squeezed. Thomas woke up then, but I don't think he recognised me at all. He soon passed out again. A new poultice is on his leg and I'm here recovering some calm.

Do I send a message to Aetherius and tell him "horse boy" is here? Would I tell him if it were a stranger? I mean, I would tell him, but would I send a special message? Not if I felt safe, so this isn't different, is it?

I let the salt air kiss my cheeks. It's not like I need to decide anything this minute. He's going to sleep through the night, I hope. His fever needs to break and that cut on his leg needs to drain before it can heal. Zara nuzzles my hand, having given up on the rabbit. "Alright, sweet girl. We'll go back."

We step in quietly and I hear his breathing is steady and even. I heat up water for a cafe and then sit with a book, but my mind isn't on it. I stare blankly at the same page, deep in thought. Eventually, I decide not to send any messages today or tomorrow, but on the third day I will. By then, Thomas should be heading back home. His horse seems fine, so she'll be strong enough to carry him. I'm not keeping it a secret from Aetherius, but I don't need him, so there's no need to cause a bunch of man-egos to get in the way of healing.

Would I be ok with Brigid doing that? Actually, should I send a word to her? Really, what would she be able to do? If I send word, she'll just hurry here or send someone to fetch him and what he needs is to stay still. Tomorrow maybe, I'll send word to her that he is recovering and will head home the following day. That has her not worrying but also no need to come "rescue" him. By then, I should know how he ended up in these woods in the first place. Travelers rarely come close to here, that's why I like it.

I sigh and blow a strand of hair out of my face. Why does it feel like I'm keeping a secret I shouldn't?

Later in the night, Thomas began tossing and turning, speaking gibberish in his dreams. But some cold chamomile tea dribbled down his throat, and peppermint leaves, crushed then slipped in his cheek, seems to sooth him and eventually he falls soundly asleep again. A few hours later when I wake his skin is cooler to the touch, and the cut is only warm, not hot. His body is strong, he'll be fine.

I sleep a little later than normal, and surprisingly, Zara lets me. It's an hour or two past dawn when I go out and check on the mare. Lady is her name, I gathered last night. So I give Lady fresh water and then let her out of the shed to eat the grass by the cottage. My feeling is that she won't wander off.

I turn to go inside to make some breakfast and startle. Thomas is leaning in the doorway watching me.

"You shouldn't be standing," I scold him.

"It is you." He shakes his head and rubs his eyes. "I thought it was a dream, but you really are here."

"Well, it is my house."

"But..." Thomas trailed off, clearly confused.

"C'mon, back inside and sit before you fall." I push him back into the cottage and towards the table. "You fell off your horse, back in the woods. You were fevered and very ill. Zara brought me to you."

"Zara?"

"My wolf."

"Oh, obviously. Like Skye."

"Yeah, they're old friends."

"Right."

"Anyway, your horse helped me drag you here. I couldn't lift you back up. But we brought you here, cleaned you up and took care of that cut. That's why you had the fever."

"Cleaned me up?" Thomas looked down as if just realizing he was wearing a stranger's clothes and turned beat red.

Ignoring that, I asked, "Do you remember how you were cut?"

"It was storming badly, and I fell. But it was when I got some mud in it that made it worse, I think."

"You did have some nasty smelling mud on your pants."

"Sorry."

"How does it feel?"

"Sore, but...not bad. But where? Why?" Thomas kept starting and stopping. "Thank you."

"I couldn't very well let you die in my woods."

"Why not, the witch would."

"The witch?"

"You know, the mad woman living near here."

I lifted an eyebrow.

"You haven't met her?"

"I haven't *met* her, no. We live quite contentedly here." I only put a little emphasis on met and waited to see if he figured it out.

"Oh," was all he said.

Yeah, braun not brains here. But Light, he was still gorgeous! And I knew his body felt perfect under my hands. Imagine what it would feel like under my lips.

I busied myself making breakfast then, so he wouldn't see my flush.

Chapter 26 - Thomas and Brigittia

I can't help but watch her. She's so strong and sure. And by all the gods, she is gorgeous! I can't imagine how amazing she would look on horseback.

Thomas had woken up again, but this time Brigitte hadn't noticed and he had time to watch her. He was feeling better. He knew she had saved his life. Now he was content to stay here, under a blanket, and watch her in the kitchen. Soon enough she came to sit beside him carrying two mugs of cafe. Apparently, she did know he was awake.

"Here," she offered him a steaming mug.

Thomas propped himself up on his elbows and sipped the liquid. It was deliciously warm and harsh, but heavy with cream and sweetness.

"I don't know how you usually drink your cafe but you should have the extra honey. It will help you heal. The cream will help give you some energy, too."

"Mmm. It's delicious, thank you."

"Do you feel like something solid to eat? Porridge this morning probably wasn't that satisfying."

Thomas considered his options. He was hungry, but he also enjoyed the coddling she was giving him. "If I say yes, will you spoon feed me, still?"

She scoffed, "No, I scolded you for walking about this morning, but you're more than capable of feeding yourself."

"Hmm, I wish I were feeling up to more." He grinned, "To show my appreciation, of course."

Brigitte blushed. "Of course." Her heartbeat sped up even as she berated herself that anything like that with Thomas would be a terrible idea. Once she had thought that they were fated mates. Now, she knew better, but...Light he was so attractive.

"So... we last saw each other the morning after the ball. And it was crazy and chaotic." Brigittia spoke slowly.

"Traumatic even," interrupted Thomas.

"Yes, traumatic. Indeed. Did you know anything to expect before you arrived?"

"No! Did anyone know?"

"Well,..."

"Wait, you knew??"

"I knew parts. I knew it culminated with marriage. I just didn't realize- I didn't expect, I mean-"

"Uhhuh," Thomas took pity on her and interjected. "You knew you would get married, but didn't know you would have to consummate it?"

"Yeah. Or be watched." She laughed uncomfortably at the memory. "And we can't even warn the next guests. Unless you were there, I can't talk about it."

"I know! I tried to tell my best friend and the words just stick in my throat. It's awful."

"Yeah."

They were both silent for a moment.

"But," Brigittia asked softly, "are you happy with her?"

"Yeah. Yeah, I am." Thomas held her eyes. "I really thought you were my partner. Guess I'm an idiot for that. But she's good to me."

"Good."

"Yeah. She's expecting our first child soon."

"Oh." Brigittia blinked fast. "Good, she always wanted children."

"Yeah, yeah, I guess." Thomas rubbed his thumb against his chin. "Yeah, and my herd is doing alright. Actually, that's why I was out. I was going to get more colts. But then there was the storm, and we went under the trees to get out of the heavy rain and...I don't know. We both fell down a bank and I got lost."

"And you cut your leg and almost died."

"Yeah."

"Ready to send her a message? We should let her know you're alright and you'll head home tomorrow."

"I will?"

"You'll be fine to travel then. She shouldn't worry about you, but she needn't send anyone for you either. You'll be fully fit to ride all day tomorrow."

"Oh." Thomas was grateful to be almost healed, but disappointed, too. He was enjoying Brigittia's energy again. He didn't want to leave yet.

Brigittia stood up and hurried into the kitchen to avoid looking at Thomas any longer. She knew he needed to leave. He was married to her friend, for Light's sake. But she liked having him here. And she kept imagining his arms around her and his lips back on hers. They had only met at the ball. They had only kissed at the ball. He had only held her at the ball. But it had been a magical night together. She had been so sure he was her riddle partner. She had been so sure the fated mates' markings matched. She looked down at her wrist, looking at the vines.

They were not matches, and it didn't matter what she had thought. She had been wrong and now they were here at this moment. She stepped over to the desk and withdrew paper and ink.

"Here, write your message while I make us a salad." Then she whirled back to the table and sliced fresh bread to go with her fresh greens and the berries from the day before. She sawed at the crust a little harder than necessary.

"Thank you." Thomas stared at the paper, unsure of what to write. Eventually, he decided to just give basic information and not say that it was Brigittia who had rescued him. He could always explain that in person. But he was pretty sure he would keep it as his own secret. There wasn't any reason that Brigid had to know. But a little seed of doubt grew in his mind and sprouted into his heart. He should tell her, but what if it upset her? And being pregnant, she didn't need extra stress. Right? Right, he was being considerate to keep this secret. He deserved to have something just for him. After all, there was nothing illicit about this.

My dearest Brigid,

I'm sorry to worry you. I had a slight accident befall myself and Lady, which has delayed us. I will be traveling home in two day's time. We are both fine, now - do not over-worry.

Depending on the weather, I'll see you the evening of the third day or by midday the next. I hope you are well. I am sorry to have been gone for so long.

Love, Thomas

Thomas had fibbed a little on the letter to Brigid about how long he would be staying away. Brigittia saw it and didn't correct it before sending the letter off. Thomas didn't know if she knew or not. They were wreathed in secrets.

The next morning Thomas leaned in the doorway, watching Brigittia rubbing down Lady. She was comfortable around horses, but also clearly didn't have the right equipment. Still, her intentions were apparent and Lady appreciated the attention.

Thomas walked up behind Brigittia and murmured, "Here, she really likes when you rub right here between her shoulders and then scratch down through here." As he spoke, Thomas wrapped his arms around her, sandwiching Brigittia between his body and Lady.

Brigittia couldn't help but smile at the flirtation as she adjusted how she rubbed and scratched Lady. At first Thomas rubbed Lady too, his hand right beside Brigittia's. Then his other hand settled around her waist. Brigittia leaned back against his chest and turned her head to ask, "What are you doing?"

"I, I, I don't know." Thomas gave a shaky little laugh. "This feels right though, doesn't it?"

"Yeah," admitted Brigittia. But then she took a deep breath and stepped to the side, breaking out of Thomas' touch. "But we're both married."

Thomas leaned his head against Lady's neck. "I know."

Brigittia focused on calming her breathing. She tried to reach the calm she used when she practiced with a sword.

"I know we're married to other people, but I still feel like we should have been married," said Thomas softly. "This feels right. Why else would I have gotten here with you?"

"You're here because you were hurt. I couldn't heal you out there-"

"No, but why did I get hurt? Why did you find me? Why your woods? Why your cottage? Is this fate?"

"I think Brigid would disagree."

Thomas reached out, grabbing Brigittia's hand and pulling her close. He tipped his head down and kissed her berry colored lips.

Brigittia stood stiff at first, but it felt so right. Her lips parted, and she kissed Thomas back. She looped her arms up behind his neck. He slipped a hand into her hair and held her tight.

They kissed hungrily for a few minutes and then they stumbled back and into the cottage. Thomas switched from holding her tightly to running his hands all over her body. In return, Brigittia pressed tight against him and slid her hands up his back, over his strong arms and shoulders.

Without a word, they began removing clothes, gently at first and then roughly pulling, tugging, and a button flew wide. They both panted a little in between kisses, their lips grew swollen and their teeth bumped. They giggled through it and soon were a tangled mass of arms and legs on the blanket Zara had quickly abandoned.

She scratched her nails along his chest, twirling through his curls. He shivered as her hands traveled lower, and he gasped as she grasped him gently, squeezing. He pulled her over on top of himself. She straddled her legs around his hips and put her weight on her arms. She dipped her head low to lick a nipple, which grew hard under her tongue. He groaned and then groaned again as she slid down, continuing to flick her tongue down his smooth skin. He was a golden tan, and the skin goose bumped as she went. She slid her hands along the side of his balls and then her fingers grasped him again and guided his cock to her lips. She licked around the head, and then she ran her lips down the length of his shaft.

Thomas moaned and rested his hands on her shoulders. She tensed and paused for a moment, but he didn't move further, so she continued. She ran her tongue up and down the vein of his cock, then slipped it in her mouth, swirling her tongue around the head. His fingers tightened on her, but he neither pushed her away nor pulled her closer. She began taking him deeper into her mouth, pressing and holding her tongue against the vein as she used her hand to guide him in and out. He was rigid in her mouth, his whole body taunt, and then he convulsed slightly as she bumped his cock against the back of her throat.

"Oh yes," he moaned.

She continued moving up and down, stroking her fingers to follow her mouth. Then she shifted her weight and pushed his legs apart. Once he did, she reached her other hand down to hold and stroke his balls.

"Oh goddess, you are amazing."

She chuckled, earning another moan." I'm not." She said between strokes.

"You are."

After enjoying her another few moments, Thomas gently pushed Brigittia back and pulled out of her mouth. He flipped her over and spread her legs. He had apparently learned a little from women before her and quickly located the center of all her nerves. He gently flicked and then swirled his tongue around her clit, causing her to gasp. He gently pushed her leg a little wider, keeping a warm hand on her inner thigh, and then set to licking steadily and firmly. After a moment, he paused long enough to lick his finger and then he began rubbing it around and then inside her as his tongue continued its dance.

Just as she wasn't sure she could survive not feeling him on her and in her, he looked up and grinned. "Good?"

"Uh, yeah!" she laughed softly, "but I want more. I want you inside of me."

Obligingly, he slid up on her, holding his weight up with his powerful arms. He dipped his head and kissed her lips, still swollen from their kisses before. She reached down and stroked his cock, then guided him into her. Thomas slowly pushed in and then pulled almost out before pushing back in. They held each other's eyes and smiled. Brigittia lifted her head and met his lips for more kisses. Thomas began thrusting faster, and she bucked her hips to meet him thrust for thrust. Soon, they were both glistening and breathing hard. Thomas pulled back and hesitated, then thrust long and deep as he came. Brigittia moved her hips up and down a few more times, grinding against him. Then he collapsed on top of her, careful not to crush her, and they both panted.

"You're a goddess, I tell you." Thomas grinned and then pulled out and off of Brigittia rolling to her side.

"Hardly," she snorted.

Chapter 27 - Brigittia

"Travel well," Brigittia stood by her fence and patted Lady's neck.

"I'll come back soon," said Thomas.

"No," Brigittia spoke softly but firmly. "You can't come back."

"Why? What do you mean?"

"You can't come back. We shouldn't have done this. You go home and you don't come back."

"But...but why?"

"We're married, Thomas. We never should have done this."

"But it was-"

"It was." Brigittia smiled. "But we shouldn't have. Aetherius may not care, I don't know. I'll talk to him soon. But I know Brigid won't be alright with this. She has every right to be angry at us."

"She never has to know!"

"That's up to you, whether you tell her. But I know. And I know she wouldn't be alright with it." Brigittia stepped back as Thomas tried to grab her hand.

"But I love you!"

"No," said Brigittia sadly. "You love the idea of me. We enjoy bedding each other. But we don't love each other."

"But, I-"

"Go home, Thomas."

"No, but I-"

"Go home, Thomas. Go home and forget me." Brigittia smiled at him, then turned and walked back to the cottage, ducking around the side. She leaned against the wall, breathing heavily. It wasn't love, it was lust; the emotions were powerful regardless. Brigittia didn't want

Thomas to leave. She didn't want him to go home to Brigid, but she knew it was the right choice.

Aetherius wouldn't be upset with her. They had talked extensively about open marriages and polyamory and the impracticability of arranged marriages, especially secret ones. But there were two 'buts':. But she didn't love Thomas, Brigitte thought ruefully. But also, she had the nagging feeling that she had been neglecting something.

Brigittia took a deep breath, then wiped her hands as if wiping away the past with a few swipes. She pulled her hair back, coiling stray pieces behind her ears, and turned onto the path to the cliffs. The salt air strengthened her convictions further and calmed her emotions. She whistled for Zara. They began to walk along the cliff beside the forest to where her typical journeys ended. Along the boundary of where she typically went, Brigittia placed a wall of wards. Thomas wouldn't find her again. Zara added her own markings as they went. As she walked and worked her magic, the itch between her shoulder blades slowly eased. This was her calling. This was her nature being true. She needed to be in touch with the natural energies.

By lunch time, Brigittia had made a full circle back to the happy cottage. She smiled when she saw Aetherius lounging in the sun, waiting for her.

He shaded his eyes as he felt her approach, and grinned at her arrival.

Brigittia bit her lip, then asked, "Do you want to talk about it?"

Aetherius had felt her weaving wards and had sensed the horse boy's fading presence. He understood what she was doing. "Only if you want to."

"Will you think less of me if I don't want to?"

He laughed then, "Absolutely not! Remember, I've been around for a few centuries. We've all had our dalliances and our play. Our choices make us in the long run, but not every single choice is world shattering."

Brigittia smiled. And this is why she loved Aetherius. They were partners and friends, as well as lovers.

Brigittia dropped down on the steps beside him and closed her eyes, tilting her face to the sun. "Have you been busy?"

"A bit more than I anticipated," acknowledged Aetherius. "I think half the reason I'm here is to relax and nap for a day or two. I'm exhausted." He leaned back onto his elbows also. "I need to leave again soon."

"Want some lunch?"

"We could make lunch."

"Good, I'm famished."

"Hiking will do that to you."

"Mmm hmm. And magic."

"True. Cafe too, then."

"Oh, that sounds heavenly!"

"Cafe is good anytime."

"True!" They both laughed. It was one taste they both enjoyed everywhere they traveled, exploring new flavors, and always returning to their favorite brews. And just like that, they settled back into routine.

As they ate lunch, they chatted about this and that. He waited until they were cleaning up to mention the mentor. "I may have found someone who can teach you more than I."

"Oh?" asked Brigittia with delight.

"Mm hmm. She's a lovely woman and I think you'll like her. She's a tad...sarcastic, too. She's direct, she's kind, and she likes hard cider. Like you, she's a warrior and a healer."

"Alright, she sounds fun to hang out with."

"She's also powerful. She knows a lot about the auld magic, ley lines, and so many things that I have only heard about."

"Yeah?" Brigittia hesitated. She felt a '*but*' coming.

"But," he flashed a grin, "you knew there was a catch."

"I did."

"But she spends most of her time in another realm and is very, very busy there."

"Another realm? Alright, so traveling would take time."

"Well," Aetherius hedged, "not actually."

Brigittia lifted an eyebrow and waited.

"Yeah, her distant realm is really, well, alright, here's the deal. Queen Arichel lives in a parallel world. She is a fae. But she also Travels between worlds, so she can easily Travel here. Hmm, we may need to change some of your wards, but she can meet you here. You just have to understand that she isn't always available."

"Queen?"

"Yeah, but she's not pretentious."

"Uhhuh. And she would be willing to teach me. She doesn't have...queenly things to do."

"Yes, and yes. Yes, she does, but yes, she is."

"How do you know her?"

"Actually, I only just met her. But my brother knew her and asked her. Apparently, she often teaches those who find their magic and are untrained."

"Hmmm."

True to his word, a few days later, Aetherius arrived at the cottage with a stately woman. Queen Arichel had the same warrior's pose and calm as Brigittia, but the power emanating from her presence was astounding. Then she stepped closer and her aura was warm and welcoming. Brigittia immediately felt as if she had known this red-haired, piercing blue-eyed woman for her whole life. Arichel hesitated a moment at the gate of the path, but as soon as Brigittia smiled and welcomed her, she hurried down the path and embraced her as if they were cousins who hadn't seen each other for months.

The first afternoon, Arichel stayed and chatted for a few hours, but then left again. She had just wanted to meet and get a feel for each other first, she explained. "I think we'll get along just fine, don't you?" she asked.

Brigittia grinned and answered, "Oh, I think so."

"I have a gift for you, as well," said Arichel. She handed Brigittia a little cat shaped gargoyle. "Her name is Bast. She'll help guard your house from pests."

"She's sweet," said Brigittia, examining the minute details of the statue.

"She's something. I'm not sure she's sweet, though."

"No, she's adorable," argued Brigittia. "Look at the attention to detail in this. I swear she could just start purring in my hand."

"Indeed."

Brigittia found a cozy spot in the sun and set the cat down. Stepping back, she said, "She looks just like she's guarding my door."

"Mmm hmm. She is."

"She's like a good luck charm? Or, carries a ward?"

"Bast is a little more complicated than that, but holding a ward is a good way to think of her. I'll teach you more about her and similar things next time."

"Now, tell me more about what you do know. I'm sure you had tutors growing up." Arichel sipped the cider as she spoke. "This is delicious, by the way."

"Thank you, my aunt made this batch. Umm, my tutor spent a lot of time teaching me the histories, and government theory, as well as basics of geography, reading, and writing. I had a sword master too, who taught me a little."

"A little?" Arichel raised an eyebrow and smiled wider.

"Maybe more than a little," agreed Brigittia. "We also did a bit of hand to hand."

"Mmm hmm. Poisons?"

"And antidotes."

"Good. Obviously, you know how to cook and sew as well. Do you make tinctures?"

"I know a little about herbs and healing."

"Good. When I come back, I need you to not be modest. I need to know when you already know something and when you have questions."

"Yeah." Brigittia understood, but paused in discomfort. "I'm used to downplaying my knowledge, but yes, I can see how you need to know what I know so you can see what I don't know. I think that I don't know far more than I know."

"That's alright, we all start somewhere. Has anyone taught you magic?"

"I know a little to draw wards on my body and to create some wards nearby."

"Do they last for long?"

"As long as I want them to."

"Really?"

"Umm, yeah."

"Do you need to renew them, ever?"

"I have to repaint the ones drawn on me."

"Mmm hmm. If they were inked, would you need to?"

"I, um. I don't think so. I have some that are inked on me, and they have never been redone."

"Hmm." Arichel seemed thoughtful at this. "I will try to come back soon. You have wards up. Can you change them so that even if you don't see me, that I may enter your garden or better yet, come onto your porch in case of poor weather?"

"You can't now? But I didn't let you in?"

"You did when you smiled in welcome to me. That was effectively you welcoming me in. But I think it was temporary."

"Yeah, let's do that."

"Good. I want to show you some basics and see how much power you really do carry."

"Alright."

"You're special, Brigittia, and the auld blood is strong in you. I have other duties, but you are now one of my priorities. Maybe not next time, but soon, I think I will bring a good friend of mine as well. She knows more about poisons and gem work than I do. I think you might learn some from her as well."

"Alright, but..."

"But?"

Brigitte flashed a rueful smile. "But I can't help but feel like I'm not this special."

"Oh, but, child, you are."

Brigittia chewed her lip at Arichel's words.

"But you're a queen. You must have more important things to do."

"No." Arichel shook her head and then tucked a strand of hair back. "No, I think you are perhaps one of the most important people on the continent. We just don't quite know how yet."

The End

Author's Note

Author's note:

I very much hope you enjoyed this story! If you enjoyed this story, you might also enjoy Parallel Worlds [1] and The Ancient Ones[2]. You can find all of my stories here on my Linktree: https://linktr.ee/ authorrachelroy. I would love for you to join my reader groups on Facebook and/or join my early access on Ream! Never forget that authors love to hear from you, so please reach out by email or social media.

Thank you for your support and have a wonderful day!

Rachel Roy

---

1. https://www.amazon.com/Parallel-Worlds-Rachel-Roy-ebook/dp/

   B0C83MXKMR?ref_=ast_author_mpb

2. https://books2read.com/u/bWYyMD

Preview of In Blood We Trust (not yet published)

Episode 1 -

We get a bad rap, y'know, but literally we were born into these families just like other paranormals were born into theirs. The only difference is that I can choose to Turn someone into the family instead of Marry them into it. Same thing, just mine is forever, there's no divorce except for beheading or a silver stake through the heart (no, not wood, not if you want to be sure). Sunshine hurts us, garlic is gross, silver is what is painful, but you take the head off any living thing except a worm and you pretty much can be sure you killed 'em. I kinda wonder why metal collars aren't a fashion statement with us.

So, let me take you into the scary underground world of vampires, actually I hate being underground, but you get the idea.

First, let's get you settled as my guest. You'll have to trust me as we travel through the Gates, but by all means, let someone know where we're going so you know they can send a rescue party. I'm fine with that. No different than the rescue text on a blind date. I get it.

So we're gonna travel through the gates to my place. No it's not a haunted mansion or a gothic castle. It's actually a really nice condo in a laid back community. We have a whole mix of paranormals and shifters there so it's really very non judgemental and easy going. There's a spare room you can stay in, with a real bed and everything. I don't sleep in a coffin either, by the way. Tonight we'll go to my friend's restaurant. He's a vamp too, but he can cook the best damn steak you'll ever eat. Tomorrow we'll have breakfast at the Shifter Diner - spoiler, it's a bunch of shifters who work there. And you'll want a firm grasp on your wallet because the clientele is rather...shifty. No loose jewelry either.

I had to do some fast talking and make some heavy promises but then you get to come with me to the casino. There you will pretend to be my understudy, do you know anything about poker? Texas Hold-em? You'll spend the evening with the heavy players. There will be a variety of species playing and suddenly they don't have a problem with vamps when they want to play our games or borrow money from us.

Yeah, anyway. We'll see how you're feeling then, if you want to tag along for a second day. Sound good? If you're too scared, or this isn't what you want, now is the time to back out. No harm, no foul. I'll make sure my cousins know you left with no animosity between us. But truthfully, and I'll always be brutally honest, truthfully, I really want you to come see our world. See how we are shunned for actions that fairytales have made up. Stupid storytellers. Taking "little liberties" and making up "small details" to make the stories "better". Then somehow all the fae are amazing or haughty and aloof, and vampires are sneaking through shadows, hanging out with bats, and preying on innocents. Although the stories do give us good looks and superstrength. Too bad the shadow hopping isn't real either. About the only thing those fairytales get right is the intelligence. I will say that both vamps and fae believe in educating our young. Plus we live a long time, so we end up pretty darn intelligent.

"Ok, ready? Let whomever know that we're going through the Castle Draug Gate today. Tomorrow, we'll travel through the centaur's gate at House Briarthorne. He lets me keep a car there to drive into the city." I consider it a minute, then add "I'll go over there and grab us a couple coffees while you make your call. Give you some space. How do you like your coffee, or would you rather tea?"

Episode 2

WE WALK THROUGH THE Gate like we own the place. In a way I do. These Gates, these Ways of Travel are built of the old magic. It runs in my blood. A lot of us have the old blood, even among the humans, most of them just don't talk about it. One early summer day leads to another seamlessly. We walk along a stone paved path, past the benches for the readers and people watchers. Then down the little hill alongside the water and out under the trees and arch from the park. Suddenly, we're in the middle of a small city. I guess it's more of a suburb right here, but I like it. My condo is just down the road from here, an easy walk. Almost everywhere I want to go in this city is an easy walk from my condo. Tonight we'll go a little farther to reach the steakhouse, that's downtown, but everything else is almost within sight.

My little follower is pretty brave for a mortal. I gave her plenty of opportunities to let her people know where I'll be taking her. I want her to trust me. I want her to be able to share our side of the story, so to speak. Sure there are bad vamps. There are bad unicorns, too. But most of us aren't.

We walk in silence down the path, under the arch, and down the street. "It's quiet here," she comments.

"Yeah, that's why I like it, I guess. It has everything I want to live near, but it's not crazy busy."

"Hmm."

"Here's our turn up here." I point up to the wrought iron fence. I see her eyebrows lift a little even though she doesn't say a word. "Iron is a myth. Like fae promises. Just some good details for a story." I grab onto one of the pickets of the fence for effect. Luckily, she just nods and looks away. I flex my fingers a little. Iron doesn't burn us. It's almost the opposite actually, my fingers are stiff like they got really cold, but the effect wears off almost immediately.

Here I am talking about being honest and blowing it in the first ten minutes. But I wanted to show her proof, albeit a false one, that story details are not always true. And truthfully, not all vamps are affected by iron. It seems to only be a few of us that share some ancient DNA from the north. I dunno, but it was worth the moment of discomfort.

Her eyes widen seeing a medusa walking our way. "Hi Lilith," I nod to the woman. "Just don't meet her gaze, look at her ears or her neck or something," I whisper to my new friend.

I hear her grunt a reply to me, and then a barely audible greeting to the gorgon as she walks by. They are a little terrifying the first time you see one with all her snakes writhing about. Lilith is a bit of a free spirit, and the only time I have seen her trap her little vipers down was when she covered them all in a very large hat on an unusually snowy day. I am sure it was only to protect them, not from any societal pressure.

"Remember, there are a variety of species who live here. When in doubt just smile and look at their shoulder. I'll keep you safe if you do something stupid unintentionally."

"Uhhuh."

"No really, it's a chill group of people who live here. We're all so different, we all just live and let live, y'know."

We walked up the path to my door. Actually it's a door into an entrance hall and then my door inside there. "Just a moment, I might still have a 'begone' ward aimed at humans, let me check so I can disengage it." I forgot about that, this morning.

"Why do you ward against humans?"

"Actually, I ward against almost everyone. I like my quiet. But the wards have to be set to specific species or attributes. They all are basically the same though, encouraging the visitor to go away." I wrinkled my nose at the smell of cabbage soup coming through the air. "Sorry, the troll has developed a taste for cabbages. Come on in."

"Troll?"

"Yes, why?" I asked closing the door.

"Trolls are real? I thought they were just made up monsters under the bridges."

"There are a few under bridges I dare say." I wish this one would cook his cabbages there. "But no, generally they're right here with us. Many do use a little glamor to um...smooth their features. Their size is notable, but often they masquerade as football players or such. My neighbor apparently plays rugby."

She giggled, "I see."

I kinda like her.

Episode 3

"WHAT ELSE IS REAL THAT I don't know."

"D-uhh," I rubbed the side of my nose, "I really have no idea how to answer that since I don't know what you think you know."

She laughed again, "True. Nevermind then."

"Well, no," I said, "That's really kinda the crux of why you're here. I want you to know what's true and false, so we need to eliminate the fallacies these stories are built on. C'mon, let's sit in the kitchen." I led the way down the short hallway to the bright kitchen.

She blinked a little coming in. For some reason, my sunflower themed kitchen always surprises visitors. She stared for a moment at the little fountain gurgling on the counter.

"I used to have one just like that. The fountain, I mean, not the cat."

I stood frozen in surprise. "You can see her?"

"Well yeah. I love gray tigers."

"Me too." I walked over and picked up the bundle of fluff. She stretched out, arching her back and yawning so wide I wondered if her mouth could flip inside out to swallow her head. I rubbed behind an ear and a rumbling purr started. "However, most people can't see this fluffball. This little monster is actually a hellcat."

"Yeah, right," she laughed, and then stopped looking at me. "Are you serious?"

"Oh yes. She will grow up to be one of the most fearsome hunters in the world." Which was hard to envision as she had now dug her sharp claws under my arm and was hanging from the underside of my elbow, rumbling purr even louder than before.

"But she's...adorable." The little demon's head popped up over my arm. She gave my thumb a quick sandpaper lick and then she leapt right for my visitor's shoulder. Somehow she caught herself and precariously turned around. I couldn't help but wince as I imagined the feel of the claws gripping into the shoulder to stop her sail through midair. A hiss was all the human let out. Tough girl - no doubt. And then the kitten started nibbling the human's ear.

"I've heard of hellhounds, but not hellcats. Well...maybe I have actually., but-"

I groaned, "But you've only heard about them as a derogatory description of a feisty woman." I shrugged, " Not entirely inaccurate, although insulting. She's just a kitten, imagine how ferocious she will be later when she's all grown up."

"Umm, yeah." I looked over at her from the coffee I was making. The kitten was thoroughly licking her ear. She did that to me once. The rumbling purr is disarming until the sandpaper hits the inside of your ear canal and then you're torn between pleasure and pain.

"That is a unique sensation, isn't it?"

"Uhhuh." Her voice sounded strained, and I empathized. "Her tongue and her purr combined were a weird mixture of pain and pleasure. You can pull her off, if it's too much."

I figured the mortal could handle my hell kitten for now, she was handling everything else well. So I said, "How do you want your coffee and then let's work on more of these myths."

"Um, cream and sugar, but not too much sugar."

Again she surprised me. Mortal girls seemed to always like sweet frufru coffee drinks.

"Coming up. Cream and a little sugar." I slid the mug onto the counter beside her, then I sat down at the table. She could stand or she could come sit, there was plenty of physical space and I wanted it to be her comfort choice. "Tell me your favorite myth, let's start there."

"Umm, ok we talked about hell cats and hell hounds. So what is hell? Or where is it? Which version is right?"

"Ahh, that is a good question. And you're not going to like my first answer....It depends."

She groaned and I grinned.

"Yeah, well," I rubbed an ear, the scab itched from my last kitten bite. "SO it depends a bit on your religion and your version of the Afterlife. For some people Hell is all about demons and brimstone torture. This is actually just a small piece of hell where torture actually occurs. How you get there varies whether it is the lowest level or the center level. Then there is the idea that there are multiple levels and some of those levels have you 'paying for your crimes" if you will and then you move on to more comfortable levels. If we go all Viking then there are many Afterlife worlds each ruled by a different deity, some airy and summerish, some fiery, and some winterish."

"Where do vampires go in their afterlife since you're basically immortal?"

Dang she asks good questions.

Don't miss out!

Visit the website below and you can sign up to receive emails whenever Rachel Roy publishes a new book. There's no charge and no obligation.

https://books2read.com/r/B-A-EEVR-NZRID

BOOKS 2 READ

Connecting independent readers to independent writers.

Also by Rachel Roy

Watch for more at https://www.authorrachelroy.com.

About the Author

Rachel Roy lives in the Northeast Kingdom of Vermont with her husband and children. She has been writing for as long as she has known that people could create books. In 2021, her first children's story, Growing Up As Fairies, first appeared on Kindle Vella in serial format. After edits and illustrations she published it in print in December 2022. In the meantime she added six other series to Kindle Vella including another children's story, two non-fiction homesteading resources, and several fantasy and fantasy romances. Rachel also teaches middle school Humanities as she continues to write.

Read more at https://www.authorrachelroy.com.

www.ingramcontent.com/pod-product-compliance
Lightning Source LLC
Chambersburg PA
CBHW022119170626
46808CB00002B/777